WATER

OF LIFE

Darcy Drummond

Published by Saron Publishing in 2018
Copyright © 2018 Darcy Drummond

Water of Life is a work of fiction. Names, characters,
places, events and incidents are either the products of the
author's imagination or used in a fictitious manner. Any
resemblance to actual persons, living or dead, or actual
events is purely coincidental.

Previously published in 2003 as *Eau de Vie*

Cover images © Author

ISBN-13: 978-1-9999871-4-5

Saron Publishing
Pwllmeyrick House
Mamhilad
Mon
NP4 8RG

saronpublishers.co.uk

Follow us on Facebook or Twitter

Water of Life

Also by Darcy Drummond

Summer Season

DEDICATION

For Swanswell

Thank you

ACKNOWLEDGEMENTS

My love and thanks to Penny Reeves for helping me bring this story to life. It is a piece that means many things to me and lay dormant for a while. I spent some of my happiest years in Talloires and the surrounding Haute Savoie and I hope I have bestowed upon it the justice it deserves. Many of my friends from show business are trained ballet dancers and they inspired one of the characters in my story, so my thanks to them especially. For research I did dabble in the world of clairvoyance and mediums and found it fascinating. I'll let you know if anything I was told comes true!

Unable are the loved to die,
For love is immortality

Emily Dickinson
1830-1886

PROLOGUE

With glass in hand, slowly swirling red wine from the Savoie region in which he lived, he watched the mountains. Soon, the sun setting across the lake would bring a pink glow to their barely snow-capped peaks, producing the renowned Les Montagnes du Rose. This magical event transformed the sprawling dark hulks into awe-inspiring jewels of rose quartz, bestowing delicate beauty upon those which exude brutal menace. Only the powerful creative hand of nature can produce such anomalies.

Armand's most treasured mountain was Les Dents de Lanfon, rising majestically above his small chalet house. An old loyal friend keeping watch over him, always there, unlike Sophie. Unlike the love that had touched him all too briefly. A love he had willingly been consumed by, encouraging and nurturing it, revelling in the intense sensations. Then it was gone.

La vie, qu'est-ce que c'est? Life, what is it? A simple question for those who had a command of it and contentment in their lives, whether through family, career or simply a state of mind. They would answer confidently. For many, still striving to be something, with somebody special and probably somewhere else, their answer would be less forthcoming.

Then, there were those like Armand, who would not accept what life had dealt him and move on. Maybe, they had actually had all they ever wanted. Needed. Their *raison d'être*. That cruel and unusual creature that life can be, it is ripped away and they are left devastated, empty and wary of going forward once more.

Armand poured more of the soft fruity Gamay, comforted by the familiar sound of wine meeting glass, small things that enabled him to be calm with his constant rampaging thoughts. In his solitude, Armand could negotiate through them to precious memories, easing them out from the dusts of time, revealing moments in unblemished light and letting them warm his soul.

A chill in the air brought him back from his retrospective travels. The springtime sun had set, his old friend illuminated no longer and the wine bottle empty. Armand looked across the field to the family farmhouse. He was late for supper and he anticipated his mother's wrath. She insisted they all sat down together, and woe betide the one that wasn't there on time. Tonight though, the evening would have a different feel for him. He had made a decision.

Soaring above Perroix, a small hamlet on a large plateau above its mother town of Talloires, paragliders ascended above Les Dents de Lanfon and La Tournette mountains, filling the morning sky with a carousel of colours as they floated in silently-controlled patterns, individual pilots testing themselves, turning seemingly impossible horizontal circles. Tandem flights for those learning or tourists exploring the sport and an experience never to be forgotten. Paragliding or *parapente* was born here and only on rainy or the worst winter days were there no canopies in the air. Armand understood only too well. He too had taken his courage in hand and flown with the birds, rising like the eagles. The sensations had never left his senses and he smiled at the recollection, lifting his face to the gentle morning sun. It warmed his classic Gallic features.

He downed his shot of Ricard and slammed the glass onto the table as if making a statement. A long deliberate intake of fresh alpine air preceded a final but fleeting moment of regret. No more could he settle for this diminished life. He had tried and failed to find the inner strength that his family and friends had told him he had within him.

They turned to their Roman Catholic church for solace in times of trouble. Reconciling themselves with the teachings and lessons of their Lord while suffering through His 'plan' for them. Armand had earnestly tried to gather up his tattered faith. He knew such love that he had shared with Sophie was divinely given but it was also snatched away and that had destroyed him. Armand was uninterested any longer in what the Lord planned for his life. He had held onto what he could of the love and life he had found with Sophie and he wanted to covet it forever.

Felix Xavier, known as Fix, secured the additional harness to his friend and adjusted the strap of his safety helmet. Satisfied, Felix stepped into his harness attached to the canopy, giving everything a final inspection, double-checking all the lines were lying correctly for take-off. Everything was in order and ready to go. He reminded his charge of the sequence for commencing flight and attached Armand's harness to his own. A quick check of the wind direction and strength and at the appropriate time, he shouted a strong command to Armand to run and assist in pulling up the canopy.

They were airborne before they reached the edge of the mountain side, ascending quickly on the excellent thermals, over the pine forests below. Soon they reached the point where the tree line met with the jagged vertical rock of Les Dents de Lanfon, the wolf's teeth. From there it rose up, a giant grey monolith dominating the skyline. Circling below them, a pair of golden eagles, enjoying the thermals and casting their eyes over the land beneath for prey, glided effortlessly and with immense grace, despite their power and threat. Armand admired their serenity and envied their freedom.

Cold air rushed past him and apart from the occasional beeping of Felix's barograph flight computer, it was the only sound. The views beyond of the lake were as breath-taking now as when he had flown before. Armand looked across to the ancient old town of Annecy, nestled in the north west corner of the lake, a thousand years old and still thriving. The thirteenth century chateau and prominent Basilique de la Visitation stood proud on the hillside above. Everything he had been, everything he had become, began here.

They turned to the sound of air adjusting in the canopy cells. Ahead lay the southern end of the lake, with a backdrop of possibly one of the most stunning mountain sequences in the French Alps, the impossibly blue green waters of the lake below them. Armand saw none of it, only her face. Large azure blue eyes set within her natural beauty. Luxurious chestnut hair falling in waves, creating a perfect frame. Sophie.

'Nous avons dit pour toujours, mon amour.' *We said forever, my love.* It was just a whisper but Felix heard him.

'Everything ok?' he asked.

There was a sudden movement from Armand and Felix tried to see what the problem was. He saw his friend holding something and was struck with horror.

'Armand!' he shouted. Felix thought he heard his friend say something else but couldn't catch it.

Before the desperate pilot could react, Armand had severed the passenger harness.

CHAPTER ONE

Present Day London

Anna listened politely to the rabid gossip passing between the other dinner guests. She was a dab hand at looking thoroughly interested in a conversation when really, watching paint dry would have been more welcome.

It was the laborious training she'd had through years of company breakfast meetings, usually in the quietly opulent surroundings of the Basil Street Hotel in Knightsbridge. All present would be asked for input. But Anna knew that suggestions from the company's mere minions who were actually in the front line, like her, and knew what was needed to improve their service, generally got side-lined by the middle managers and thus, another wasted very early morning. The sumptuous breakfast fare and excellent coffee was the main reason for going.

At an appropriate pause in the chatter, Anna excused herself to join her dearest friend in the kitchen. She simply could not listen to the conspiratorial claptrap any longer. Catrin turned as Anna closed the kitchen door and laughed quietly.

'I wondered how long it would take you!'

'Ugh! I love them to bits but really... Change the subject!' Anna sighed, then looked daggers at her friend, who was trying to hide a sneaky Gitanes cigarette in the sink. 'And what's that, madam?' Anna enquired like a stern headmistress catching out a naughty schoolgirl, which of course, they had both been and giggled about often, trying to outdo the other.

'Oh, shush! Ok, I'll put it out. Don't tell Stephan, will you?'

'Of course I won't...But you owe me!'

'Always!'

Catrin took coffee and liquors to the table where the vitriol was now getting heated after the diners's liberal consumption of wine. She asked if they had everything, all gushed yes and how wonderful the meal had been, and Catrin returned to the kitchen. A quiet Schnapps with Anna was in order.

'So, how are you doing, darling girl?' Catrin asked.

'Oh, you know, same old same old,' Anna replied, then took a good glug of her brandy.

Following the dreadful events of March four months before, when Anna's husband and soulmate, Max, had died, life had been the strange and very individual episodes of grieving. Never quite the same for anyone and yet all experience trauma, despair, fury, anxiety and then utter emptiness, before, surely but slowly, starting to build a new life. Anna felt she wasn't quite at that stage yet. What hadn't helped was that Max died intestate. The awful process of sorting that out had kept her busy but now everything seemed to be in place with the right people and hopefully it would be resolved sometime soon and she could move on, financially anyway.

'So, same shit, different day, then?' Catrin responded in her soft Swedish lilt, cigarette re-lit but still held by an open window. Easy to get rid of the evidence before Stephan returned from his business jolly with some important clients.

Anna just loved her friend and laughed. 'Yes!'

At her desk the next morning, with a rather heavy head, Catrin and her 'Oh, just have one more with me...' to blame, Anna knew she needed a lot of coffee before meeting her first client later. The feeling she had was the same as going to school on the Mondays during her GCSEs and straight into double maths. Simply unfair and spiteful.

She politely called him 'The American Banker'. Mr Michaels was from New York and head of a mergers and acquisitions capital investment bank that had just opened its London office in the City. He was looking for a townhouse in the best area of London for himself and Mrs Michaels. Anna suspected he would have taken most of the elite properties she had shown him over the last week but obviously the lady of the house was more pedantic and just plain difficult. Or just American.

Going to the safe to collect keys to the next selection of abodes, Anna saw her colleague Natalie arriving for work.

'Mr Michaels again?' she enquired.

'I'm afraid so,' replied Anna. 'Another pointless troll about London. Wish his wife would actually come over and see them for herself.'

Natalie gave her a look and said with raised eyebrows, 'You really think so? I would suggest you've got the better end of the deal with Mr Michaels!'

'I suppose. Just really not in the mood for him today.'

With that, Anna left to get her car. She found it with a big plastic-covered yellow ticket slapped on the windscreen. *Oh, thanks for that,* she thought. *All I need.* Then had an image of where she wanted to stuff it.

As always, Mr Michaels presented himself with absolute style. A sharp expensive suit, silk tie and extremely shiny brogues. All topped with the whitest smile of perfect teeth.

The first property was a definite 'no'. The 'drive on to the next' once pulled up outside was the clue. So, onto

Chester Square in Belgravia. It had only just come back onto her books with the owners off to Hong Kong for two years and Anna felt this just might be the one. The square housing several embassies and an occasional retired Prime Minister might just appeal to Mrs Michaels. Her husband was the first to see the property. It was hopeful, he actually wanted to see inside.

Typical of the area, Chester Square presented as a large square of spacious terraced townhouses with steps up to the palatial front porches. Private gardens filled the centre and, although in central London, were quiet. In brief, it was about as 'on the right tracks' as she could get for this client. The house had a special place in Anna's heart. While showing it a few years ago, Anna had stepped out of her car to find a new penny on the pavement. Not long afterwards, she had taken an impromptu visit to Battersea Dogs and Cats Home, leaving with a scatty black and white lurcher cross, named Lucky Penny. Anna hoped she would be as fortunate today.

The wide, heavily polished black front door eased open to reveal a huge wood panelled hallway with a sweeping staircase ahead of them. A diamond-patterned marble floor finished the setting. Mr Michaels stepped inside, observing every angle.

'Anna, this is impressive. So far, so good,' he dazzled a smile at her.

She showed him the ground floor reception rooms, all palatial and rich in their styling and decor. Mr Michaels was quiet and thoughtful, just nodding when he wanted to see the next room. After the cavernous steel and granite kitchen, which had another smaller prep kitchen off to the side, they continued upstairs to the first floor where the main drawing room was located. All pale lemons, greys, cream and gold. It was a stunning room.

'Oh, my! Now Lauren would just love this.'

Anna just smiled and kept hoping. They finished the viewing and Mr Michaels said he would like to return with his wife, who was arriving from The Hamptons that weekend. She tried to disguise her thumping heart.

Arriving home after a very busy day, an exhausted Anna put the key in the lock and heard a familiar scampering along the wood-floored hallway. Upon opening the door, a lanky black and white bundle jumped into her arms. Lucky Penny or Slut Mutt as Max used to call her, once he got over having a dog in the house. He hadn't been keen, so Anna just came home with her. She knew he couldn't have sent her back. Penny's way of doing circles at his feet and throwing herself on her back for tummy tickles was the reason for Max's other name for her. Anna knew it was Penny's game plan to win him over.

After feeding Penny, Anna took her for a walk. Of course, this was usually done by the time she got home but since March, well, since March, nothing had been the same and never would be. Sometimes Anna took Penny to stay with her parents, collecting her the following weekend. A holiday of sorts for her hairy companion. It was becoming obvious that perhaps Penny should permanently reside with her parents but she was just not ready to let her go completely. Not yet. Too much, too soon. But her scruffy mutt's welfare and quality of life remained at the forefront of her thoughts.

One of the reasons Anna and Max were drawn to each other was their shared decision not to have children. They both believed the world was heading in a very dangerous direction and the planet's resources were stretched to the limit as it was. They were ardent conservationists, particularly where the oceans were concerned, and they decided adding to the planet's childbirth rate would be at odds with this. Many of their friends berated them in a fond, joking manner, gently counselling that they would make fabulous parents, create a beautiful child and regret not doing so in the long term. As it turned out all too soon, they never had the long term and it stung Anna every time she thought about it. She would often wonder what a child of theirs would have looked like. Max, her or a good mixture of both? Most of all, Anna had lost the chance to have a lasting impression of her soulmate in a child. To be able now to have and cherish what was half of him.

Back from their walk, Anna settled down into a deep, steaming hot bubble bath, infused with geranium and lavender oils and a massive chilled glass of Petit Chablis. With her faith still rather wobbly, this was as close to a religious experience as she could get. Apart from the expectant hairy head with dark button eyes peering over the bath edge, waiting for their game of catch the water drops.

CHAPTER TWO

Why she had agreed to the task of baking various cakes for her granddaughter's school fête, Estelle Ward would never know. She could only remember the rather bright five-year-old saying 'Pretty please, Grandmama...' so endearingly, how could she refuse? However, the agreement was coming back to bite her with floury teeth. This was the first time Estelle had baked cakes of any size or sort and what she was producing from the oven didn't quite resemble what was so beautifully photographed in the pastry cook book she had bought. However, she was no quitter and with what Estelle hoped would be a good effort in disguise with the icing, her attempts would sit proudly, if a little shy, next to those from the prolific and competitive sisterhood of the yummy mummy brigade.

Grandmama, she thought as she removed another nondescript cake base from the oven and placed it on a cooling rack. Not only had Estelle had to buy the cook-book but also an entire range of utensils, cake tins and baking paraphernalia. 'Grandmama,' she smiled to herself. For a while, Estelle had been convinced she would never be thus. Her only child, a son, had amazing career success and married late. Even then, it was a while before he broke the news that he was to be a father. It took some time to get used to the idea, although she was delighted for her son and daughter-in-law, of course. Her many friends who had several grand-ankle-biters with tales of babysitting and having them for weeks in the holidays, made Estelle quite pleased she was still at the top of her career and free of such commitments.

As she started mixing together one of the fillings, her thoughts turned to Anna Duncan, her wonderful lettings manager, who was putting a brave face on for the world, but it was clear Anna wasn't coping too well. She had lost a lot of weight and some days was positively pale and gaunt-looking, however much she tried to be her normal bubbly self at work. So young to lose her husband in such an appalling way but Estelle saw herself in Anna, for she too was a widow. Like her, when her own husband had passed away relatively quickly after being finally diagnosed with lung cancer from his smoking, which she never managed to make him give up, she had felt bereft at the waste of a life and anger in his selfish culpability. Feelings Estelle knew Anna was most likely suffering too, left alone to wade through the mire of the fall out, legal, financial and emotional. It had been ten years since Estelle's husband had left her alone. There were still moments, like the birth of little Tilly, that pulled her up short and a whisper of her original anger would waft over her briefly.

It was obvious Anna needed a complete break from everything. To recharge herself and find solace. A healing sabbatical, so Estelle hoped, would bring her back into the fold with a new sense of purpose to make something of her shattered life. There was just a hint of selfishness in this reasoning. It would be good for the business as well. Despite her valiant efforts, Natalie was far from close to being as persuasive with potential clients as Anna. So it was time to make 'that' phone call and get her plan started.

It was rare for such an early morning face to face with her boss before anyone else was in. Anna knew she'd made a few silly mistakes and had taken a lot of time off or perhaps Mrs Michaels had complained. Not that Anna could work out why, but it would not have surprised her. The woman was frankly a pain in the back side and very condescending when speaking to Anna. Mr Michaels had just mutely followed them round the house in Chester Square and as they left, managed a brief covert smile to Anna that was unseen by his wife as they got into their chauffeur-driven car.

Certainly Estelle had sounded chirpy and reassuring but still Anna's mind was in overdrive after hanging up.

'What do you think, Pen?' Anna had asked her hairy companion as she set the phone down into its hub. The dog had lifted a dozy head from her usual spot on one end of the sofa, gave Anna a brief look and settled back into her slumbers. Anna laughed quietly and then sighed, a more sombre mood overtaking her, as she felt hot tears beginning to sting. Max had spent every day after Penny's arrival, trying to keep her off the furniture, to absolutely no avail. He had even had a behaviourist trainer visit but both quickly realised that the dog, although a happy, playful and super-friendly being, wasn't the sharpest tool in the box so all further efforts ceased and a weary acceptance ensued. The recollection was quickly dismissed, and Anna wiped away the tears. When would she stop crying all the time?

The next morning, she drove into work, still surmising what the meeting was about. Whatever it was, Anna would soon find out as she knocked on Estelle's office door.

'You don't have to knock', came the response from inside.

Anna set herself down on one of the two ornate antique chairs in front of Estelle's vast rosewood desk. Another old piece that Estelle had acquired for her office, along with the sumptuous Persian rug beneath it.

'You look like a startled rabbit in headlights!' Estelle smiled. 'I told you it was nothing to worry about. Just a chat and some ideas I wanted to run by you.' Estelle sat forward and placed her chin on her hands, 'This is about you today, not work, ok?'

Not really, Anna thought. *In fact, that sounded worse!*

Estelle continued, 'I'm fairly sure I'm reading you correctly, having been where you are now myself some years ago. I know what happened to me and I see the same happening to you and I want to help.'

Anna just looked at Estelle, not knowing what to say.

'Look, I know a place you can go and be quiet and start healing your heart and mind. Now, I know when I tell you where it is, you'll think I'm stark raving mad and I accept that. However, hear me out and then let's talk, ok?'

Anna nodded, wondering what on earth her boss was planning. It was all rather bizarre so she just let Estelle continue.

'I often rent a small chalet house in Talloires, France. It's a magical place and I believe exactly where you can begin to regain some sense of what has happened. I have made some enquiries and because I know the owners well, they have held it available until I call them back later today.'

'Today?!' Anna exclaimed. 'I have to decide today?! Anyway, it's France...You know Max died...'

'Yes, Anna, I'm well aware but hear me out?'

There was a silent pause until Anna asked, 'Where is this Talloires? I've never heard of it.'

It was only now Estelle felt unsure, but nothing ventured... 'By a beautiful lake in the Alps.' There, she'd said it.

Anna's eyebrows shot up and her whole body became rigid. 'What the hell were you thinking, Estelle?! Are you serious?' she angrily spat out, instantly regretting her impolite response. 'Sorry,' Anna said, looking down at her clenched hands, consciously unfurling her fingers and placing one hand over the other on her knee.

Estelle let the dust settle, then reached forward with her hands outstretched for Anna to take them in hers.

'My dear girl, please let me explain why?' Anna took the offer and held Estelle's hands lightly, still feeling rather surprised, if not a little shocked.

'You see, it's where I went when my Henry died. A friend of mine recommended it to me, in the same way I am to you. Yes...I did consider your reaction to the setting but actually, I honestly feel you need to face up to what happened head on, Anna. It's not where the accident was but close enough. There is so much going on with solicitors and all the legal rubbish we have to go through when a loved one dies. We forget that we also need to go into ourselves and find that hidden inner strength that will help us to move forward again. It is truly a mesmeric place, Anna, just what you need, and I am very happy to pay a month's rental for you. Not a loan, a gift from me to my best girl.'

Anna gave a small nod of her head while looking off into a place somewhere behind Estelle. A lot of what had been said made complete sense, it was just the Becher's Brook-sized hurdle she had to clear before being able to accept the remarkable offer. It seemed she also only had today to make that leap and land safely on the other side.

'So,' Estelle said, getting up from her desk and walking round to where Anna sat. 'You go home and put your thinking socks on and let me know by the end of business this evening, ok? I won't be offended if you're resolutely against my idea but at least humour me and think carefully about my reasons.' She patted Anna on the shoulder as she saw her to the door. 'That's all I ask of you.'

Her decision made after much soul searching and various silent arguments between good elf and bad elf on each shoulder, Anna had made her call to Estelle as promised and then one to her parents. She was heading down to Seaford on the East Sussex coast, with the intention of having some much-needed family time and then leaving Lucky Penny with them.

Anna had accepted Estelle's offer.

Joyce came out of their house with arms outstretched, not for Anna but her hairy mate. She adored the dog and was delighted to be her guardian for a long spell. But the reason for the stay had caused a couple of sleepless nights since Anna had called to tell them of her trip to France. Despite being just the right side of forty, Anna never ceased to become her mother's little girl when visiting. It was the one place she could truly be herself, even when Max was alive, and he often found it quite amusing how girly his wife became under the fussing care of Joyce. Penny had now run into the house to find Ken. Mother and daughter held each other for a long while. Nothing spoken, just love and emotions transferring silently between them. They walked into the house and found Penny on her back having tummy tickles from Ken. Slut mutt ever at the ready. Now she was doing her circles at Ken's feet. Before Anna had reached the house, Penny already had the scent of the grasslands atop the cliffs where there was also a links golf course Ken went to most days.

Penny was now sitting, looking up and whimpering at Ken who looked at Joyce and Anna. 'I know that noise. Guess I'd better take her for a walk after that long drive. You two get settled. It's lovely to see you, Anna.' With that, he gave his daughter a kiss on the cheek, smiled his adoring dad smile and left with an excited dog pulling him out the door. Anna watched them go with thoughts about her dog's future firmly at the fore. It seemed she had yet another hard decision to make but at least there was more time in this particular case.

Joyce beckoned Anna into the kitchen where she could see through to the conservatory and her mother's usual banquet luncheon laid out ready on the table. It was another reason it was so lovely for Ken to have Anna visiting. He was allowed to feast on various foods normally forbidden by Joyce because of his high cholesterol. Penny didn't do too badly either.

'Oh, Mum, you don't have to go to all this trouble just for me.'

'Oh yes I do. Now sit down. Tea or some wine?'

CHAPTER THREE

The following day, as Anna made her way up the footpath through the farm across from the avenue where Joyce and Ken lived, she saw that the little field which had been full of lambs in March was empty. It occurred to Anna that there had been nothing but emptiness since March, when that life-changing news had arrived. She thought how equalizing life is, as a life is born, another dies in some natural continuum. The fragility of the little lambs so at odds with the monster that had consumed her husband. Could she really go there and look at the beast and find some sense in it, as Estelle had counselled?

She reached the top of the path which opened out onto the sprawling cliff top with breath-taking views out across the Channel and to her left, the famous Seven Sisters, a range of cliffs magnificent and deadly in their own way. Anna became conscious of the melodic trill warbling of skylarks hovering overhead, ground-nesting birds taking flight to warn of danger. Such as when the home phone rang late that fateful night and woke Anna who was snatching a brief weekend with her parents while Max was away, and a few moments later, her father had gently knocked on her just-ajar bedroom door and softly said her name.

'What is it, Dad?' she had replied, still sleepy, raising herself up on her left arm as he came into the room and sat gently on the bed. He leaned over to turn the bedside lamp on. Both squinted momentarily, then their eyes adjusted to the sudden light. Ken put his hand on hers.

'Dad?' Anna had said, now sensing something was very wrong. Her father's face was a mixture of things she couldn't quite put a finger on but mostly she felt his trepidation.

'I'm not sure how to do this, darling, so please forgive me.'

'What's wrong, Dad? Just tell me...Please, just say it,' Anna said, rather more harshly than she meant to, her fears increasing at an alarming rate, as was her heartbeat.

Reluctantly, Ken's eyes met Anna's. 'We've just had a call from Sebastian.'

'Sebastian?' Anna's voice caught in her throat.

'It's Max, darling,' Ken almost whispered, his voice cracking with emotion. In calm tones, he told his daughter that her husband had fallen badly during the competition he had entered. Her lover, protector, soulmate and life light was gone.

Max had travelled with his best buddy, Sebastian, to Chamonix in the High French Alps for a free-skiing competition, a test reserved for those who had reached the pinnacle of daring. A sport with a touch of danger at any level without proper instruction, but skiers, such as Max, still needed to prove themselves. Those who climb Everest say, 'because it's there'. Max would say, 'because I can.'

After being carefully placed by a helicopter on the smallest of summit ridges, Max had cast his eyes down the sheer white slopes, visualising his run. The starting gate was above a particularly difficult *couloir*, an almost vertical passage leading to the rest of the course, itself a test of courage and skill beyond most black runs. The level of competition here was the highest he had ever encountered so to truly make his mark, Max needed to seek out the trickiest path down the course while showing perfect skill and ease.

He started well, chopping and carving down the icy *couloir*. At the end of it, there was a drop off that Max executed with aplomb. The adrenaline was pulsing through him as he headed toward a large outcropping of jagged rocks. There was an easier path, but he had to opt for this if he stood a chance against the others. He was energised like never before. This would be his greatest accolade.

Max reached the ragged line of rocks and commenced a tricky traverse manoeuvre around them. Suddenly his left ski caught against a concealed rock beneath the crusty snow and was ripped away from his boot. He started to fall, knowing that going with it rather than fighting it was the best way to hopefully lessen injury, as he tumbled down the slope, gradually moving off piste and away from the course.

Max was unaware of the crevasse that lay directly ahead. A thin icy strip that had opened up in the snow and ice pack, hidden by the heavy morning snowfall. By now, Max was losing consciousness and as he dropped into the frozen fissure, his last thought was of Anna as the final darkness took him.

Despite the valiant and desperate efforts of the mountain rescue teams, by the time they reached Max's broken body, via his rescue beeper, crumpled on a small ledge within the crevasse, he was dead.

It was a while before Sebastian was informed of his friend's demise. By the time he had got over the initial shock and horror and eventually spoken to Ken, Anna's husband had been dead for several hours.

Brought back to the present by dogs barking, Anna saw two Jack Russells waiting for their owner to throw a ball. As it flew through the air, they both raced along the grassland, one jumping to catch it and then chased by the other. Anna was reminded of her decision about Lucky Penny and she sighed. Estelle had been right, she did need to get away and be at one with herself. To have peace and tranquillity to consider all the issues that lay ahead and what she would do about them. The hairy one being the most pressing.

Looking across to the Seven Sisters, Anna thought of Beachy Head, a favourite spot for her family, especially the old cliff top lighthouse, now ingeniously moved further away from the ever-crumbling cliff edge. It was also a place infamous for the desperate people who made it their final destination, leaping from the edge onto the small beaches hundreds of feet below. Her fear of heights had always meant she had never even been able to get near the edge. She considered the blind courage it must take and felt sorry they couldn't channel that courage into facing what had brought them there.

She walked westward along the cliff top and eventually dropped down to Buckle Beach, a long curling sweep of grey pebbles ended at its most western point by the entrance to Newhaven harbour. There was a constant battle with sea erosion and several large excavators were piling pebbles at the top of the beach to form a barrier in front of the homes built just across a small road from the beach. Anna sighed as she realised that her thoughts about climate change were very real and this was all just the beginning of greater, more dangerous events to come.

She walked along the beach at the water's edge and then sat in front of an old gun tower. The sea looked murky, the wind having whipped up the khaki water. Waves curled up and seemed to pause before crashing down with a rhythmic thud, ending in white foam. Each wave crept further up the beach toward her, a loud hissing as they clawed back against the pebbles. Anna watched, almost hypnotised by the awesome power. She had always been drawn to the sea, even as a small child. It had fascinated her young mind and senses and still did. It was also how she had met her husband. They were both part of a large scuba diving group on a holiday in Malta, a veritable paradise for diving. One of the group had cancelled and a new member of her club had taken their place. Max.

The sting in her eyes was no longer just the sea spray but sudden vicious tears that slipped down her face and dripped onto her hands. Irritated, Anna angrily wiped them away with her coat sleeve. It was another phase of the grief process, anger and rage, which, if channelled properly, could be very constructive in her new life ahead. Not that Anna had that in mind at that moment.

'Why?!' she screamed at the sea. 'Why?! Why wasn't our life together enough?! What was it I couldn't give you?' Anna collapsed into heart wrenching sobs. With a piercing screech, a herring gull took flight from pickings on the beach. 'I just don't understand,' she said, calmer now but still lying on her back with tears dripping into her ears. 'I just don't understand.'

Sitting up, Anna picked up a small pebble and threw it into the sea. Then another and another, then forcefully a handful, watching them disappear into the churning water as her fury subsided, as it always did, eventually. As a feeling of emotional fatigue fell heavily over her, Anna hoped going to France would be exactly the tonic Estelle had said she needed.

It was time to lay the ghost to rest.

CHAPTER FOUR

Natalie checked the document for a third time. He would no doubt still find something to be added, removed or altered. This was the second draft. In her experience, certain clients elongated the drawing up of a letting agreement to silly lengths but if it got them in the property, they would play along. Numerous phone calls, emails and missed lunches until the thing was signed and sealed.

This particular contract would most likely be scrutinised by several people before reaching the client himself, corporate lawyers at the top of the list and then one very picky wife. Natalie smiled as she imagined Anna's reaction upon learning about it when she called in to say her goodbyes later that morning.

Estelle was waiting for Anna when she arrived, everything organised. All tickety boo, as she liked to say.

'Come on in,' she gushed. Anna sat down where she usually did, on the chair to the right, she always did and never knew why. 'You may rest assured I have told no one down there about this. That's up to you, although I would be inclined not to, if you want to get away without having to go through every reason and detail with them, lovely as they are, of course!' Estelle handed Anna a large folder of some considerable weight. 'It's all in there, everything you need.'

'Gosh, thorough as ever,' Anna laughed.

'Without fail!' Estelle purred, feeling very pleased with herself for getting her plan to this point. When Anna had accepted, she had danced a celebratory jig around her desk.

The chalet had been booked for one month from the coming weekend. There was also an option to extend with good notice. The folder contained maps of the route through France from Calais, with several of the best auto route stations shown, and one for the Haute Savoie region where she would be staying. The journey with stops would take about seven hours, once Anna had negotiated Paris. It could have been bypassed but Estelle thought it would be a nice little addition to the journey, although Anna would have to find her way round the *peripherique*, the equivalent of the M25, though Estelle smiled at the thought that the much-hated British road was cast as the hero against this Parisian villain.

'No turning back now, then,' Anna said with a smile while sifting through the paperwork. 'How did you manage to secure the house so quickly?'

'Aw, well, that's because my friends and I have rented it many times through the years and are now quite close to the family who own it. They also live in the village, well, own the village, really. Three generations of farmers. The French like familiarity and always would prefer someone known to them than strangers, particularly as it's a very close-knit community.'

'I'd better cram some French. I got my GCSE but only just. Max used to do most of the conversation when...' she paused, 'we went to France...together.'

There was a long silence as Estelle let Anna regain her composure, then caught Anna's gaze and handed her an envelope. Anna opened it and found a wad of euros.

'I can't take this. You've done so much already.'

'See it as a bonus of sorts. Did Natalie tell you the news?'

'No? What news?'

'Mr Michaels finally signed the agreement. For the whole two years.'

'Oh, my God! That's fantastic!'

'So, please, see that small offering as a bonus for all that good work.' The small offering was 500 euros. 'And not to sound like a certain advert but you're worth it.'

When Anna arrived home, she felt excitement beginning to build. In just a few days, she would be setting off on her own little adventure. She wondered if Max would have been proud of her. Without thinking, she stooped to refill Penny's bowl, then stood just looking at the bowl, realising there was no tail tapping her leg and hearing the silence *sans* hound in the house. Maybe it was time she got used to it for the sake of her dear companion, not to mention the happiness it would bring her mum and dad.

Her mobile rang, and she checked the caller display, then smiled. Evidently the family bongo drums had been booming loud and clear. It was her brother, eager to know all the details of her trip. As he was saying goodbye, her brother suddenly said, 'I'm so pleased you're doing this. We've all been so worried about you, Sis.'

Anna, touched by this, was silent for a moment. 'Thanks, bro,' she eventually said, 'I love you.'

Now it was time to visit Catrin and Stephan to say her goodbyes to them. Catrin was making her famous Swedish meatballs accompanied by all culinary things Scandinavian, which Anna adored.

Later, completed stuffed by delicious fare, she stood in her spare bedroom looking at her previous attempts to pack. There were clothes strewn on the bed, hanging along the walls on pictures and various cases open at the ready.

Definitely a possible for the Turner Prize and display in the Tate Modern, Anna thought. She had never been a great case packer and had left much of it to Max who would do both sets of cases with almost military precision. His motto was always the six P's, a well-known military mantra of 'prior preparation prevents piss poor performance'.

Anna had tried her best with prior preparation but it didn't seem to be working. Then her eyes found a photo of Max, on a chest of drawers, him standing in wet scuba gear and looking very smug about the deep dive he had just completed that day in Malta. It wasn't long after his dive buddy had taken the snap that he had asked Anna out for a drink, away from the usual nightly gathering of the whole group.

They had been inseparable from that evening.

'Oh, Max,' Anna sighed but no tears came this time. She gently caressed the photo, stroking his image through the glass. 'If only I had been enough for you.'

And there was the crux of the matter. Anna knew the answer, no woman could have been 'enough'. A woman he may have been able to live without, his adrenaline highs and beer-fuelled dopamine chill downs he could not. Perhaps in time, he might have explained his need of such things but now he never could and she would remain with conflicting reasons of her own.

Their whole relationship had been based on a mutual respect for each other's freedoms. To stifle would have damaged. She knew their love was exceptional. No man had ever stolen her heart and entire life in the way Max had. Then there was the passion for everything in their shared life. A passion that was inexorably linked to his need for extreme tests for himself and whilst Anna had silently admired the way he had attacked life, he was never perfect, who was? But he had made her into a better person along the way.

Looking deep into his photographed eyes, she said, 'I'm coming to find out about you now, though, Max. I have to know why. Be ready for me.'

For everything he had brought into her life, for everything he had made her as person, she has willingly allowed this side of her beloved husband to cohabit alongside them. Thus, since his death and the turmoil she was now going through, it was never far from her mind that in some way, she too was culpable in his demise.

CHAPTER FIVE

Even for July, it was sultry. Not that he ever felt the warmth.

Swallows buzzed in the sky above the garden. Their wings iridescent blue, shimmering in the sunlight as they flew their graceful dipping dance. He knew the air was filled with their high-pitched twittering. To know this was to hear it, for he heard nothing.

His sister Josephine swept the steps to his terrace. He watched from his quiet place. She always carried a sadness about her, and it pained him. He knew what it was to feel pain. Sometimes when they were together in the house, his sister would talk to him. He would be near to her, within reach, watching her sorrowful face as she spoke.

Adjusting the front door mat and moving the two pots planted with lavender and rosemary to give a wonderful scent, Josephine left with a quick glance around the lovely garden. On occasion, he would catch her looking toward his quiet place as she took her leave, a hint of a frown on her face as she softly shook her head. Afterwards his sister always walked a little slower as she left.

Alone again, Armand watched the swallows as they caught insects on the wing. In the distant sky beyond the lake, heavy gunmetal clouds were brewing. A lively storm would come that evening, bringing much-needed rain to the farmland. His farmland. Often, he would stay in his quiet place, beside the giant fir tree in a shady corner and watch the rain as it greened the flora. Renewing life.

He knew about life but to know it was not to feel it in his solitary dreamlike state.

CHAPTER SIX

This was a nightmare. Her exit for Lyon was in sight and she was in the correct lane, if only she could get as far as the exit. As far as Anna could make out from the illuminated signs above the *peripherique* over the last seven kilometres, there were road works and now an accident in the reduced lanes. What annoyed her most, was the incessant beeping of horns. Whilst obviously quite normal practice for the Parisians, it was completely pointless but also very annoying, especially as the most prolific horn beeper was right next to her.

Just chill, babe. The words seeped into her mind as if Max had been sitting beside her. Anna smiled, took a deep breath and turned the radio up. It seemed this particular station was a big fan of the late Johnny Hallyday, the French Elvis, and it wasn't difficult to understand why.

After a snail pace advancement, she finally turned onto the next part of the journey and sped toward her destination. As the songs filled her car, Anna began to relax and recalled the conversation she'd had with her mother in law, Eleanor, before departing. The poor woman had taken her son's death just as badly as Anna and had not coped very well either over the last few months. Only now she seemed to be getting her life back together, though it would never be the same again for either of them. Anna considered whether, if Eleanor had been a stricter and more guiding mother to Max, maybe her son would not have become the thrill-seeking man he had been.

Max was Eleanor's youngest child, born some years after her first and second sons, so was truly her 'baby'. He was a thoughtful, happy, artistic and expressive boy, with a formidable temper at times, but in Eleanor he had a strong ally against the rest of the family, especially his father. A dour, regimented man, not much love remained between him and his wife. A typical scenario of staying together for the children and saving face in their social circles. Therefore, with her eldest living in Australia and the other a busy commercial pilot, Eleanor's sorrow was destined for a long duration.

After telling Eleanor about her trip, Anna waited for the reaction. Eleanor always said just what she thought, so Anna was surprised by the silence at the other end of the phone.

'I'll be thinking of you.' Eleanor eventually said. 'All my love.'

Anna stared in disbelief at the silent phone. Something wasn't right but Anna put it down to Eleanor's grief, made worse by the destination, and decided not to dwell on it.

Paris, as wonderful as it was from the *peripherique*, had taken its toll and Anna pulled into one of the service stations Estelle had recommended. It was surprisingly better than any she had reluctantly pulled into on British motorways and with a delicious *croque monsieur*, a very sumptuous ham and cheese sandwich, a double espresso and some chocolate, Anna sat in her car and looked through Estelle's folder. Suitably refreshed and after an interesting visit to the loo, a tiled cubicle with a hole in the floor and getting the timing right to flush the whole area before getting soaked, an amused Anna set off again.

At Mâcon, she turned due east toward Bourg-en-Bresse, famed for its gourmet poultry. From there, her journey would wind through massive gorges until the outskirts of Annecy, where the mountains rose up to form the classic alpine scenery. By the time Anna arrived in the chic resort town, she was exhilarated but exhausted. Noticing the hotel on the lake's north bank that Estelle had listed as worth a visit, she headed there.

Seated on a delightfully sophisticated terrace above beautiful manicured gardens, she looked out across to the lake. A coxless four was gliding through the mill pond waters, leaving a gently widening ripple behind them. Anna sipped her *coup de Champagne* and acknowledged once again, Estelle had been spot on, this was undeniably stunning. When she had accompanied Max on skiing holidays in France, they had driven from Geneva airport straight to the resorts, such as Chamonix, Val d'Isère and her favourite, Courchevel, bypassing this enchanting place. Her sadness grew that she was now here without him.

Returning to her car, Anna checked the map for the route to the house. It was located in a small village above the bay of Talloires, halfway down the eastern side of the twenty-two-kilometre-long lake. Tempted to stay for another *coup* in the rich ambience of the Hotel Imperial, she decided time was of the essence, the light was fading and it was only fair to the landlord to collect the keys at a timely hour. Besides that, the champagne was working its magic and Anna felt another would not be conducive in her search for the house and in any case, she would definitely be over the alcohol limit.

Passing the picturesque alpine villages, she felt a new sense of calm befalling her. The area had a serenity that would lend itself perfectly to rehabilitating a troubled heart and mind.

As the car began to climb the hill out of Menthon-St-Bernard, there was a brief glimpse of a fairy-tale chateau and an awesome landscape. Trying to keep her eye on the road rather than the amazing scenery before her, she saw a sign for the village she needed and turned off the main road. Standing proud and defiant against the twilight blue sky ahead was Les Dents de Lanfon and below this, the imposing mass of Perroix.

Estelle had given very detailed instructions as to how to find the house as there were no numbers or named properties, only the American-style post boxes at the entrance to each. Anna drove through the village lanes and finally, having looked at the photo Estelle had provided, came to a stop at the house. She slowly drove onto the gravel driveway and gazed up at it.

Beyond anything she had imagined, the chalet house was simply gorgeous and Anna began to cry. Perhaps it was a continuation of the realisation she had at the hotel: Max was not here with her to share it. Composed again and as instructed by Estelle, she walked up the small road to another chalet house and knocked on the door. Two young boys came running to peek through the glass panels, jabbering in incomprehensible French, then a very attractive woman opened the door, shushing her boys back into the house. She looked at Anna with a startled expression, scanning her face. *Have I got a smudge on my cheek?* Anna wondered.

With a lovely smile, the French woman indicated for her to come in and she found herself in a rustic but perfect, cosy alpine home. The two boys, one with his thumb stuffed resolutely in his mouth, stood watching this strange lady.

Madame Gilbert took some keys from a drawer in a magnificent wooden dresser. As she approached Anna with them, her eyes once again seemed to scrutinise her face.

'Here are the keys,' she said, handing over a sizeable bunch. 'Go and settle in and I'll come down tomorrow to check that everything is all right.'

With a handshake and friendly smile, Madame Gilbert said her goodbyes and Anna walked back to the house. She couldn't wait to see inside but after finding herself on the raised terrace by the front door, Anna viewed the garden. Commanding the farthest corner was a spectacular fir tree. Anna imagined it being lit up on a Christmas evening, bringing twinkly light to a winter garden and providing wonderment for any resident children. Upon entering the house, it did not disappoint.

Despite the lingering summer heat outside, the interior was cool, most likely due in part to the ceramic-tiled floors. Having collected her cases from the car, Anna decided to open a celebratory bottle of wine at the table and chairs on the terrace. She sat looking up at the slab of grey mountain that cut a sharp status in the skyline above the village. It may have been her tired state or the soothing wine she sipped but Anna was sure the huge rock was turning an illuminated shade of pink.

CHAPTER SEVEN

Something stirred in his silent world.

A tremor disturbed the vacuum.

Then he saw her.

It was as if all lost time was suddenly reinstated and his longing for her was unbearable.

He cried out, the intensely desperate wail of a man who had drawn breath, but his scream of sorrow had been denied for eternity. Unfulfilled desire surged through his form, he was alive again and his love had come home.

CHAPTER EIGHT

'Arrêtez!' Madame Boniface shouted. The dogs were being particularly annoying this morning. It was such a still and peaceful dawn as she tended her hens and collected newly-laid eggs, some still warm. Bird song, especially that of her favourite *le merle*, a blackbird, lightened her spirit, and the reassuring squawks from the cockerel, a local prize-winning specimen, brought a smile to her weathered features. All of this was welcome within the natural ambience. Barking dogs definitely were not.

'Allez! Cherchez Jacques,' she ordered the two Labradors, who ran off towards the fields to find their master. It would give Marie the peace she craved these days, after a life tending the land which she loved. But now, at her age, there were times a quiet moment was necessary. All her life, she had lived in harmony with the farmlands. Her father had been a respected farmer and, in keeping with tradition, she had married another farmer's son whom she'd known since childhood. Jacques had grown into a strikingly handsome man. Although there were several suitors through the years, Marie had always intended to become the wife of her Jacques.

Before that could happen, WWII broke out and consumed their lives. Jacques had watched as the Nazi cancer had spread its diseased tumour throughout his beloved land, and wanted to join *la resistance*. He was thwarted by his young age and later the need to work the farms with so many local men having been lost. He kept an eye on Marie throughout and hoped she would still be free when times were kinder, and he could properly court her.

Jacques and Marie were married, uniting two formidable farming families, and produced a son one year later. Armand. An heir to carry on their work nurturing the small piece of beautiful land within the Savoie region. Divided into two parts, or *departments*, Haute Savoie and Savoie, its people known as Savoyards, had a colourful history. For several centuries, the whole region was Italian-ruled, the capital being Turin, just a short distance away through the Mont Blanc Tunnel, carved deep through the mountains between the two countries. In 1861, after many negotiations with Napoleon III, the Kingdom of Italy was established by King Victor Emmanuel II and the Savoie was returned to France.

During WWII, the region gave rise to some of the fiercest resistance in France, holding off the approaching German army for a long time by securing the mountain gorges through which Hitler's soldiers needed to pass. Eventually though, the might of the invading military blasted its way through and many brave men, young and old, perished. To this day, their memorial cemeteries and gardens, of which there are many in the Alps, are places of local pride, looked after with love and gratitude. To visit them gives a stark sense of their sacrifice.

As Marie reminisced, Jacques pulled into the courtyard on his ancient but still functional tractor, preceded by two slavering, panting hounds. He had spent the day turning lines of hay to make sure it dried to perfection in readiness for hay baling later that evening. He had hoped, in vain, his son would have taken over the responsibilities, enabling him to slowly relinquish the reins and enjoy a semi-retirement. Jacques would always have kept a hand in somehow, it was in his blood and he would rather drop in a field than die in a chair. However, that was not to be.

Many times, Marie had thought about her impetuous and passionate son. He had been a taller, more ruggedly refined-looking man than his father. A stubborn loner prone to deep thought and yet, having a lighter, practical joker side to him also. Like his father, he had delayed in finding a bride and Marie felt this had been his mistake. Unsure and confused about such things, it had compounded his downfall. When someone did enter his life, the wrong woman, a transient city dweller, his fate had been sealed from that moment.

Jacques never spoke of his son. The pain was etched deeply in his aged eyes, chasms of unbearable anguish and resentment. Whilst Marie suffered the torment of her son's untimely death as a motherly duty and let it become part of her being, watered down by time, it remained an eternal entity within her shattered heart. She was of stern no nonsense stock so of course she carried on. What else could she do? A sense of purpose she wished above all else her troubled son could have achieved.

After breakfast, Jacques rested while Marie made her way down to the vegetable garden to gather ingredients for lunch. As she carefully selected the best produce, placing them neatly in her old basket, she saw a young woman watching her from Armand's house. Josephine had told her an English woman was renting her son's house on recommendation from Estelle. Marie had grown very fond of Estelle and trusted her judgement. Even so, she felt unease when seeing this new woman, not that she understood why but the feeling was quite profound. You silly old woman, she silently berated herself.

Anna sipped coffee as she watched and admired the aged but obviously very capable woman harvesting her vegetable patch. It was heart-warming to behold. In a wrap floral country dress and straw hat, the woman appeared physically frail and yet there was a youthful grace in the way she methodically dug and harvested, placing the produce carefully in a basket.

Downing the rest of her coffee, Anna recalled the vivid dreams she had woken from. Not able to recall any details, she still found them strangely unsettling. However, never mind that, it was time to explore Talloires, the mother town further down the mountain and set on the banks of Lac Annecy.

It was everything that Estelle had enthused about and more. In fact, it was as close to paradise as Anna had ever felt. Set perfectly on the edge of a most scenic bay, once honoured by the delicate brush strokes of Cezanne, was the Père Bise, an exclusive hotel at which, Estelle's handy information advised Anna, the Duke of Windsor, later and briefly King Edward VIII, John F. Kennedy and Richard Nixon had all stayed. It was not beyond the simplest imagination to see why such a calibre of guest would not have been out of place.

A rumbling stomach prompted Anna to drive into Annecy and stock up the bare cupboards. Madame Gilbert had provided bread, milk and coffee for which she had been grateful but now it was time to see what she could find on her first ever trip to a French supermarket. Max had always made sure their accommodations included a chalet girl. Essentially a housekeeper, and usually British.

Josephine decided to call upon the English lady, to make sure she was happy with everything and in case she needed any help to settle in. Finding the house deserted, she sat at the table on the terrace. Her gaze settled on the giant fir tree, planted by her brother as the finishing touch to his newly-sculpted private park. Now it had grown into the fine specimen he knew it would, having chosen this type of fir so that it would mature and embellish his garden as his wife and child would his life. Alas, in the end, he never saw the beauty he had so lovingly began.

For as long as she lived, Josephine would never understand, let alone come to terms with the devastation her brother's final act had cast upon the family and many of those throughout the community. The pilot who had flown with him that day could never manage to open his canopy again. Something within him had died that day, too.

Josephine's only hope was that their God was as forgiving as they had been taught, even though his sin was one of the gravest of all. Maybe now her brother had found the peace that had so eluded him in life. It was a luxury none of them would ever have again. Her father was forever a changed man, always with a haunted look in his sad eyes, once vivid green, now clouded by the unspeakable memories of the day his son ruthlessly stole his *joie de vivre*.

A persistent tugging at her skirt eased Josephine back to the terrace. Philippe was asking to sit on her lap while Patrice was fast asleep in his pushchair, thumb-sucking in his sleep. Time to leave. She would call back later and bring her mother, as was normal for all new guests. As Josephine got up and started toward the steps of the terrace, it suddenly felt as though there was no air or sound, as if time was suspended, then a chilling sensation of a cold breath moved past her. It faded instantly but the experience had felt as real as the prickling on her skin as tiny hairs stood on end.

By the time Anna had unpacked the shopping, she was once again exhausted. She remembered it always took a day or so to acclimatise to the fine mountain air. She decided a hot croissant with a good helping of the pungent creamy Reblochon cheese of the region would be in order, washed down with a chilled Evian water. Afterwards, she stretched out on the sofa and promptly fell into a deep, satisfying sleep, oblivious of the almost undetectable disturbance in the air around her.

The net curtain at the window above her head moved, seemingly brushed by a gentle breeze. A small strand of hair which had fallen across her forehead wavered, as though delicately blown by the softest of breaths, while the tips of his fingers tenderly traced the familiar features of her peaceful face.

CHAPTER NINE

Trying to put Penny in the bath was to attempt to put a square peg into a round hole. That was if you could catch her once she became aware of your intentions. With all four spindly lurcher legs splayed out stiff as planks, she was finally lowered into the bathtub, as Joyce laughed quietly with images of Spot the Dog in the *Woodentops* drifting through her thoughts. After several gentle requests were ignored, Joyce pressed firmly on her rump, and Penny sat, ears flat over a thoroughly hangdog expression. All of this would have been unnecessary if Penny hadn't chased after and then flirted outrageously with a very handsome Cavalier King Charles called Louis. With their sparring and Penny rolling onto her back in front of Louis, she had obviously found fox or badger scent. Just as Joyce got Penny's coat thoroughly wet in preparation for a good shampooing, the phone rang.

'Oh, for heaven's sake!' she exclaimed. She threw a large bath towel over Penny and said sternly and with much annoyance in her voice, 'Now stay there!'

Angrily pulling off her rubber gloves, Joyce snatched up the phone. 'Hello!' she said in a huff.

'Oh...Erm...Is that Joyce?' a refined male voice enquired.

It was familiar. 'Yes, this is she.'

'Hello there, Joyce, this is Sebastian.' Too familiar.

Joyce had little time for this man. To her, he was a partner in crime with her now-deceased son-in-law and also to blame for her daughter's grief. Personable with impeccable manners, there seemed something about him that Joyce could never reconcile. Barge poles and trust were never far from her mind.

'Sebastian, to what do I owe the pleasure?'

'I understand Anna has popped over to France for a while.'

Hmm, where was this going?

'For some desperately needed peace and quiet,' Joyce said, hoping her message was loud and clear.

'Well, she left me a message before she went and I wonder if you could give me her mobile number? I seem to have mislaid it. I would love to catch up with your daughter and see how she is, well, you know...' He trailed off.

Oh, Joyce knew all right. She had always known. Not an interfering mother generally but carefully counselling her children throughout their lives, she tried not to make judgements and trusted they would learn their life lessons and make their own decisions. Sometimes though, it was too difficult to let an opportunity pass.

'I spoke with Anna yesterday, Sebastian. She is well and settling in. The place is beautiful apparently and the rest away from everything here will do her the world of good.' Joyce tried again to get her message across. 'Just as long as you understand that.'

'Of course, of course, Joyce. I want Anna to be well too. It's just we haven't spoken since... When...' Sebastian wavered momentarily then recomposed himself. 'I would just like to reconnect with her.'

On that, Joyce reluctantly gave him Anna's number.

She found Penny in the middle of the bathroom floor amidst an array of sodden towels, one clamped gamely in her mouth. Her very guilty eyes met Joyce's. Then she started scampering about the bathroom, tripping over the towel dragging underneath her. Joyce could do nothing but laugh at the stupid dog.

'Anna certainly got a right nutter when she got you. Now, young lady, give me that towel.'

Sebastian spoke to Anna's message service. He ended by saying he would call her again. Since learning of her travels to France, he had felt compelled to speak with her. It would be the first time since the funeral. It had been almost too awkward then between them, very little was said only the necessary condolences and gratitude for them. After that, Sebastian had found ways to completely avoid his friend's widow because he knew, in some way, he was also responsible by helping Max enter the competition. It was his connections that had gained his friend a place. Now there had been time to reflect and Sebastian knew there was something he should have done at the funeral but he had fallen short of the man he would have expected himself to be. With distance and silence, he had searched deep within himself and realised certain aspects of his person required changes, a softening perhaps. He hoped Anna would accept those changes he had tried so hard to make, that was if she responded to his call.

Sitting with a single malt Scotch in his mansion flat, Sebastian tentatively stepped back to the edge of the abyss on that ruinous March day in Chamonix.

He had watched from the official viewing station through powerful binoculars as Max was deposited at the starting gate. It had snowed during the night, but the alpine skies were now devoid of any cloud and powder blue. The mountain slopes sparkled as though encrusted with a myriad of diamonds. Trust his friend to have this backdrop to his last-ever foray into free-skiing competitions.

They had talked at length before attending the tournament and Max knew it was time to bow out. New young talents were pushing him to the side-lines and, besides, he felt the need to give more of himself to Anna, his world, the love of his life. Max acknowledged during tête à têtes with Sebastian in their Soho private members' clubs, their favourite haunts together, that he had been greedy in his quest for the ultimate buzz, failing as the husband he had promised to be on their wedding day.

Sebastian initially decided Max was having a midlife crisis and just let his friend ramble on over bottles of champagne, followed by the occasional shot or two of something stronger. However, as time went on, it became clear Max was quite serious and Sebastian decided he must give his support if Max needed it. The poor sod had never had any real support from his father. In fact, he had become his father's nemesis toward the end, the man dismissing all things Max with venom at times, and therefore Sebastian would take his place, as best he could. Never quite sure what to do or say but hopefully his friendship and the lending of his ear was enough.

'The thing is, Seb, if anything happened to me, before I had a chance to put things right... Man... I'd never rest.'

Beyond all that, Sebastian harboured a profound guilt. His life, unlike his school friend's, had been one long playground. From immensely wealthy parents, his father an industrialist and urban legend and his glamorous mother a top socialite and charity campaigner, Sebastian had dabbled in the family business after attending Scotland's St Andrews University. But his father insisted he go out and build his own financial career and come back into the fold when 'you are a bit more useful to me'. Once the dutiful son had forged excellent skills in the City as an international investment banker, his father had finally taken notice, bringing Sebastian back safely to his side.

Walking over to the drinks cabinet to pour another two fingers of his Scotch of choice, a Highland single malt with sherry wood finish, he sighed. As the rich aromas from the pale golden liquid met with his Baccarat crystal tumbler, he knew what he had planned would be fraught with emotion but since March and even before that, thoughts of Max's wife had become something of an obsession.

Anna woke with a start. She'd been dreaming again but at the moment of consciousness, the content was entirely erased. Feeling chilled, she decided a brisk walk would help.

Clouds caressed the top of Les Dents de Lanfon, spreading billowing tendrils and reducing the dominant mountain to an apparition within the cumulus. It was cooler today but still warm compared with home. Anna looked up as she walked through the village and caught sight of the colourful canopies of the paragliders that, again, Estelle had given her information about. The woman was in the wrong job, she should have been a bespoke travel agent. Seeing where they were landing, Anna made her way in that direction, finding herself in front of a lively bar called Le Cantonnier, meaning *the road mender*, which Anna thought was unusual but she supposed even road menders need a drink after work. The bar had a large outside area, full of the paragliders but she found a small empty table and sat. Almost immediately, a barman was wiping down the table and placing a menu in the centre.

With a cheeky smile directed straight at Anna, the barman said, 'Bonjour, Madame.' He was quite tall with broad shoulders and a mop of pepper and salt hair. In fact, he was just gorgeous.

'Bonjour, Monsieur,' she replied feeling her face colouring. 'Je voudrais une verre du vin blanc, s'il vous plait.'

'White wine, Madame, of course, coming right up.' he replied in perfect English but drenched in his delicious French accent. It never ceased to amused Anna that, upon hearing you make an effort in their language, the French would instantly try and impress you with their command of English. With a smile and a wink, the barman disappeared behind the bar. Anna found herself watching him go and in that sudden surprising moment, realised it was the very first time she had noticed another man in that way since Max. After finding him, all other men had been off her radar. The thought lingered as the stirring of feelings, buried but not forgotten, lightly touched upon her innermost self with the gentle ripple of a still pool disturbed by a single raindrop.

Returned feeling much lighter in mood, she noticed there was a message on her mobile. Sebastian. She recalled her own message to him before leaving. He had been difficult to contact, obviously having changed his number, so she had spoken to his landline from hers in a last-minute attempt to make contact. So how he got her mobile number, she was at a loss. Listening to his voice, Anna was pensive. He sounded strange, not like the Sebastian she remembered. Yes, at the funeral he had been reticent and fragile-looking, but this voice suggested something else.

Anna had never blamed Sebastian for what happened but also had not had the strength to tell him that. Maybe now it was time to put that right.

CHAPTER TEN

'Coucou.' Josephine smiled as Marie Boniface sang to her youngest grandson. 'Coucou.' Patrice giggled from the pit of his tummy as all infants do, leaving even the most cynical all gooey-eyed and laughing at the cute sound. Marie held up another spoonful of mashed vegetables, and a gaping mouth, much like that of a fledgling sparrow, happily ate from it. Feeding this grandchild was never a problem, Marie mused, he was a gannet. It pleased her because Armand had been the same and had grown into a tall, strapping young man, lean but with strength and if she wasn't being too biased, a very good looking one as well.

Josephine looked across the table to her mother, having finally negotiated a small spoonful of macaroni into Philippe. This son was quite different. Meal times had become battlegrounds but somehow his *Maman* managed to get enough into him to satisfy what she felt was necessary.

'Maman?' she said, looking at Patrice, eagerly letting his grandmother put another spoonful into him.

Marie scraped remnants of broccoli and potato mush from Patrice's lips and chin. 'Oui, ma chère?'

'I shall be going to see Madame Duncan later today to check she is ok and so you can meet her.'

'Yes, I would like that,' Marie replied, not betraying her real feelings about it.

'There is something else,' Josephine said. She had deliberated delayed telling her mother this since first meeting Madame Duncan. It seemed as though she were maybe over-reacting to what she saw as an incredible likeness to her late sister-in-law.

However, her mother was old now and it might be too much of a surprise.

'Quoi?' Marie asked.

'Madame Duncan...You might think she's...Oh, I don't know...'

'Josephine, just tell me. What is it?'

'Perhaps you might find she looks like Sophie.'

There was a visceral tension in the space across the table between them. Daughter waited, hoping her mother would not erupt into one of her famous rantings when upset or angry. Mother looked at daughter's terrified face and decided it had been very brave of her to advise her so. Her own previous feelings upon seeing the woman at distance returned with a vengeance.

Marie lifted Patrice to her shoulder and got up from the table, smiling kindly at Josephine.

'We shall see, my dear, we shall see.'

After a long swig of his third Scotch, Seb decided it was now or never. He dialled Anna's mobile and heard it ring.

'Anna! It's Sebastian.'

'Hello, Seb, how are you?'

'Never mind me, how are you?!' he gushed, voice full of false bravado.

'I'm ok, Seb, thanks. Some ways to go but this place will help tremendously.' He sensed her caution. 'It's amazing, Seb, have you ever been here?'

'Where is here?'

'Talloires? On Annecy lake? Not far over the border from Geneva.'

Yes, he had been there and yes, he knew it was amazing. However, he played it down, keeping to his plan.

'No, I haven't. Is it truly as wonderful as it sounds?'

'You have no idea, Seb. I can't believe I'm here... And on... my own... Sorry, just...' Seb had the feeling she was about to end the call.

'Anna, I know. Please don't worry. Just know I'm thinking of you, ok?'

'I will, thank you.'

Sebastian took a deep breath. Time to test the water. 'Um, there is something I need to say, Anna. Do you think you might be able to listen to me for a moment?'

'I'm not sure. I'm expecting someone... Oh, what the hell? Just what do you want to say, Seb?'

Sebastian launched into his well-rehearsed speech, terrified of fluffing his lines, and yet, as if by magic, the words flowed. By the time he'd finished, he knew that they were back to some sort of friendship. Anna was quiet after hearing what Max had said about his love for her before he died, then she said simply, 'Thank you, it means so much.'

Seb could hear the rap on a door and Anna said, 'I'll have to go, it's the owner, come to see if I'm all right.'

'Anna, thanks so much for this.'

'No worries, Seb. I'll call you soon, *au revoir!*'

Sebastian sat back and drained his glass. *So far so good.*

Anna opened the door with a friendly smile on her face for Mesdames Gilbert and Boniface. The terrace was deserted.

'Officially going loopy, Anna Duncan,' she said out loud to herself, walking back towards the terrace. Shaking her head, she considered calling Seb back. 'Leave it for a while, Anna,' she told herself firmly.

She spun around in shock as another rap startled her.

She opened the door more cautiously this time, then breathed a sigh of relief.

'Bonjour, Mesdames!' She offered a hand to Josephine and then her mother, but the old lady hesitated while scanning Anna's face, then very slowly, without taking her eyes off her, Marie offered her small delicate hand. Stepping back, Anna said, 'Entrez, s'il vous plait,' and led them into the sitting room. Marie said something in fast incomprehensible French to her daughter and there was an uncomfortable pause. Josephine smiled apologetically at Anna.

'Maman isn't feeling very well. I will come back again.'

After closing the door behind her guests, Anna stood for a moment. What had just happened? Maybe it was just that she was still a bit fragile after speaking to Sebastian. Walking up on a path above the house, Anna took in the incredible vista across the south end of the lake. Although she had spent much time in the French Alps and the Rockies in Colorado, where the scenery had always been spectacular, it had never struck her as poetical as the scene before her did. Absorbing it, she had a sudden awareness of appreciating the natural world again. Until this moment, she had abandoned any beauty of nature surrounding her. She couldn't even remember the last time she had heard a bird sing, admired a sunrise or sunset, taken the joy from the little gifts the fauna and flora give us from day to day and she began to weep silently.

Marie sat at her daughter's kitchen table. Josephine set a glass of homemade lemonade in front of her mother, but she remained solemnly gazing out the window, still as stone. Then with a strange, monotone voice from somewhere buried within her, said, 'It is a sign.'

Josephine looked at her mother aghast. *Where did that come from?* Marie's voice was flat and filled with loathing. *Not like her mother at all.*

'Maman? What sign could it be? What do you mean?'

Marie's eyes met her rather startled daughter's. Her face had an uncharacteristic darkness about it.

'I must see Father Luc.'

'Father Luc? Whatever for? I told you Madame Duncan held a resemblance to Sophie...'

'Don't say her name again. Ever,' Marie snapped.

Josephine reached across the table and took her mother's hands, 'Come now, listen to yourself.'

'No, Josephine. You don't understand. She has come back.'

'Maman, please! Stop this nonsense, you're scaring me!'

Marie got up from the table and walked to the kitchen door. Turning as she left, she glowered at Josephine.

'That woman is not going to meddle with my family again!'

CHAPTER ELEVEN

Enjoying a long illicit drag on her cigarette, Eleanor closed her eyes and laid her head back on the armchair in her little den, a tiny box bedroom which she had made into her private space a long time ago. Her husband had the study for his peace and quiet and this room was her sanctuary, away from him, away from everything. Positioned looking out over the west side of the garden, Eleanor often sat and watched the sunsets and wondered what the next dawn would bring. It hadn't been happiness for years.

A car door slamming heralded the arrival of her friend, Renata. Quickly extinguishing the evil weed, she went down stairs and opened the door before Renata could knock. She made her entrance in her usual chaotic style of *mwah mwah* air kisses and warm embraces.

"Darling lady! So lovely to see you,' then she breezed off to the kitchen, leaving Eleanor to close the door and follow with a droll smile on her face. Typical Renata.

'How are you, sweetheart?' Renata asked, making herself comfortable on a stool at the breakfast bar. She ran a hand through her thick blond hair, still worn in a 1980s type of shaggy mess. An expensive one. Eleanor often wondered what her friend's annual bill was for the hairdresser in Beauchamp Place, Knightsbridge she had been loyal to for yonks.

'Earl Grey?'

'Of course! Now answer my question.'

Without looking at Renata and brewing the tea, its pungent bergamot overtones filling the kitchen with a moreish perfume, Eleanor said, 'Oh, you know, *comme ci comme ca*, darling.' She brought the teapot and cups over with some lemon slices and a box of glazed fruits, their favourite treat. Pouring the honey-coloured tea, Renata looked at her friend and frowned, realising she looked a bit withdrawn and pensive.

'What's up, sweetie? Tell Renata all about it.' She picked out a glazed orange segment. Perfect for the tea.

'Do you know of any clairvoyants?' Eleanor ventured, then hid her face behind sipping her tea.

'Do I know any clairvoyants?! Ha ha, you silly thing! Of course I know some, loads, but why?'

'I don't want you to think I'm mad,' Eleanor sighed.

'Me think you mad?! Good Lord, that would make me certifiable! What's happened? You never came across as being interested before.'

Eleanor hadn't been, until the dreams had started, sudden, graphic, waking her in the night, unable to get back to sleep in case she returned to them. By morning, she had forgotten much but random images remained which she would go over and over, to figure out what her troubled subconscious was trying to tell her.

'It's just I've been having some odd dreams, Renata. Really vivid and disturbing and I don't usually dream much. Is that something one of your clairvoyants could help with?'

'Yes, of course they can and I know exactly the best one. His name is Michael and I've known him the longest. He's quite young but I assure you he's tip top and unbelievably accurate. I'll make an appointment and. How exciting!'

Eleanor felt uneasy but smiled while Renata looked absolutely cock-a-hoop.

Climbing the ornate staircase to the second floor flat, Eleanor stopped on the first landing, and turned to her friend eagerly following behind.

'Am I doing the right thing, Renata?'

Hands on hips, Renata replied, 'Yes, you are, Eleanor, and stop worrying. Now get a move on!'

A tall thin man with neat fair hair opened the door. With a slightly pinched face but pleasant on the eye, Michael greeted them warmly.

'Renata, dear, how lovely to see you again and this lovely lady must be Eleanor?'

Eleanor nodded and stifled the sudden intense urge to run back down the stairs.

'Come in, come in, ladies! Renata, show Eleanor to the drawing room for me, lovey, *me casa su casa* and all that. I'll be with you in a moment.' Michael went toward the other end of the corridor and disappeared into a room.

The drawing room was richly furnished. Casting her eyes about, Eleanor said, 'He must be successful to afford all this, especially in South Kensington.'

'Well, he's recently recorded some shows for an American cable channel. He was invited over there by a friend. He's really getting into the big time now!' Renata said, sounding like a proud mother.

Michael returned. 'Eleanor, if you'd like to come with me. Renata will stay here, won't you, lovey? She knows the drill,' he smiled and set off down to the same room. Eleanor obediently walked behind him, her mind racing, nerves on razor edge. *What had she been thinking? Oh, it's all just nonsensical voodoo mumbo jumbo anyway,* she thought. *Just get on with it gracefully and go home.*

The room was small but also expensively adorned, with two small sofas opposite each other. The curtains were drawn and there was a soft glow from a lamp in a corner,

Eleanor felt instantly soothed by a comforting aroma of burning incense.

'If you prefer not to have the incense, I don't mind,' Michael said in soft voice as they sat on each sofa, Michael to one end of his well-worn one, and Eleanor in the centre of hers.

'Oh, it's fine, Michael.'

'I find it helps to clarify the mind and spirit. Do you have any personal items, like a necklace or a ring you are wearing? Maybe something that has a lot of sentimental value?'

Eleanor took her necklace and handed it to Michael, who patted her hand after taking the necklace into his. 'It was bought for me years ago,' Eleanor said suddenly, not really knowing why she said it.

'Excellent,' was all Michael replied, as he sat back with the necklace in his left hand, eyes closed and face serenely blank. Eleanor watched him closely and saw a gradual change in his demeanour. He gently rubbed the delicate gold chain between his thumb and fingers, then seemed to quietly acknowledge something with faint nod of his head. Michael's eyes flickered slightly, then he was completely still, the necklace swaying slowly from his fingers. The room was soundless, and Eleanor could hardly breathe. She expected Michael to suddenly metamorphose into a raging demon with goat's eyes and fire spraying from his mouth.

'Your son died recently, Eleanor. Is that correct?' Michael opened his eyes and looked kindly at her. For a moment she could say nothing. *Had Renata told him?* 'Am I right, Eleanor?' Michael enquired, rather more firmly this time but still in soft, even tones. Eleanor swallowed and tried to keep a spring of tears from developing further.

'Yes, Michael, in March of this year.' Her words sounded far away as if said by someone else.

'Your son is fine, Eleanor.' An unguarded single sob came from Eleanor and she put her hands to her face. Michael continued. 'He is still transient but safely on his way to the final destination.' He saw her bewilderment at his words and smiled. 'Sometimes we don't pass for a while. When some of us die, our soul wanders for a bit, finding its way, but eventually all seek the light and pass to the other side. I sense your son died suddenly.'

Another sob came from Eleanor. 'Excuse me, Michael, I'm so sorry.'

'Dear Eleanor, you were particularly close to this son and it has been a very difficult time for you. Let me assure you, your son has a guide and he will pass over in time.'

'Is he speaking to you? Can I speak to him?' The words were desperate.

'No, I have guides who relay information to me. Your son in his present state is unable to communicate. It may be some time before he is able. Do you understand?'

Of course she didn't, not at all, but she nodded anyway, blowing her nose into a hastily-found tissue in her bag.

'You should also know that some spirits never wish to be contacted. It can be distressing for the person seeking them but as with the living, some souls need to be left alone.' Michael closed his eyes again and became still. He seemed to bow his head and then said a very faint, 'Thank you.'

Eleanor was frowning as he opened his eyes.

'I thank my guides. They do get rather tetchy otherwise.' He became trance like again. Eleanor tried to blow her nose quietly without disturbing him. She looked around the room, it felt heavy, but not with incense, the air was definitely different. Or was that just her fear? The silence was broken by Michael.

'There is a woman here. A young woman. Do you know who this might be, Eleanor?' He was still in his trance state.

'No...no, I don't,' Eleanor said while searching her mind for a young woman whom she might know who died but there was nothing. *I'm not helping much, am I?* she thought.

'She is searching for someone. Could it be your son?'

'Not that I'm aware of. Who is she?' Eleanor thought she might faint.

'She passed over but the person she seeks refuses to. He is earthbound, a soul bonded here for a reason, sometimes fear of having done wrong in life and fear of the retribution that awaits them. Of course, there is none but many faiths believe this. They get lost and confused. Then there are those souls who are not aware they have died.'

Eleanor felt an intense heavy feeling in her chest. It frightened her. *Could this woman be the same girl who invaded her dreams?*

He opened his eyes and smiled, 'They've gone now.'

'Gone?'

'Yes, they come and go at their own leisure, Eleanor.' Michael appeared tired as he gave her the necklace back.

'Are you ok?' Eleanor asked.

'Of course, but it takes a lot out of me when a very demanding spirit comes through. I wonder, how would you feel about returning tomorrow? I want to connect with that spirit again. She was quite insistent. Do you feel able, Eleanor?'

Try and keep me away! she thought. 'Yes, same time?'

'That would be much appreciated, Eleanor, thank you.' What Michael didn't tell Eleanor was that he had to contact this spirit again because she was lingering and he needed to know what had brought her through so strongly to him.

The following day, Eleanor arrived alone. She had slept soundly that night, no dreams or nightmares. She relayed this to Michael as he showed her into the little room again.

'It's quite possible this woman was trying to contact you.'

'Me?! Why? And anyway, Michael, nothing like this has ever happened before.'

Once again, he took Eleanor's necklace. Eleanor now watched with fascination rather than fear. It felt as though a huge burden had been lifted from her.

'There is a man living...Odd...Computers? Not sure what... Ah, here she is.'

Eleanor gnawed at her fingernails. Dreadful habit but unavoidable today. Michael opened his eyes and studied Eleanor for a while. She tried to appear calm and collected. It was far from the truth.

'There is danger for them.' It was a simple statement. Eleanor felt as though she had shrunk into the sofa. Michael carried on. 'A man and a woman connected to you and yet... Maybe... I see water. A sea? A lake?'

Oh, my God! Eleanor thought.

Michael was back in the room and reached for Eleanor's hands.

'It is not usual for me to advise of such things. It is a code of practice we keep among ourselves. However, in this case, the message was off my scale of where to draw the line. I need you to let this all sink in, lovey. It's all been rather a baptism of fire for you!

'Now hear me, Eleanor, sometimes messages are mixed or I can misinterpret them. After all, I am human, believe it or not!' Eleanor wasn't smiling at his quip intended to lighten the mood.

'I know you're very good, Michael, it's only because of Renata singing your praises that I came to see you.'

'The spirit world has no concept of time. To them, a hundred years is another so-called day to them. It may be something from many years ago and is just coincidental that they have come through now. Trust me on this,

Eleanor. I want you go home and get a better perspective on our meetings. If you need to talk, please call me any time.'

Eleanor returned home and went straight to the fridge to pour some wine which she took to her den and after sitting into her armchair, lit a cigarette. What was she to do? Computers? She was pretty sure she knew who that was and Anna hadn't been far from her mind either. She decided to call Anna, to make sure that all was well with her. Perhaps it was one of the guides that Michael had spoken of or maybe it was just good old female intuition.

CHAPTER TWELVE

Sebastian watched his small bank of computer screens, alive with tables of fast-moving stocks and shares, flickering before him. It was a busy day for trading with breaking news about a huge merger between two pharmaceutical monsters, not to mention the general malaise within the British markets, with constantly changing output from the government on the current difficult economic situation. Figures were starting another downward trend, sending the illuminated numbers into the loathed red of negative.

Not that he was paying them much attention, because his thoughts were not there in his office, near his father's. He looked out over the increasing silent panic and crescendo of the electronic speculations before him, ignoring his several business mobiles beeping with urgent messages and missed calls. Sebastian focused through the wall of windows in front of him, down to the Thames and Tower Bridge. All that occupied his mind was his best, now dead, friend's, widow.

He'd kept his feelings about Anna to himself through the years because it was a lost cause. She and Max had been an irrepressible unit, only with eyes for each other. Sebastian knew he could have any woman he wanted. Except that one. His long and treasured friendship with Max was also an overriding issue. However, with their enviable union permanently severed, was this the window of opportunity he had secretly yearned for? Were the confines of respect and loyalty as relevant now, with Max gone forever? Would an approach, even with all the delicacy and consideration required under such circumstances, be abhorrent and at odds with the changed man he was trying to be?

Later that evening, completely drained from the intense trading, a considerable dip at closing and a less than cordial meeting with his father, Sebastian slammed his front door shut with a back kick of his heel. He got into the shower and with the head control on pulse action, he let the instant hot water pummel his body. Like an experienced masseuse applying a deep muscle massage, the water kneaded his skin with spiteful fingers and he could feel the tensions of the day and his emotional meanderings wash away with a satisfying gurgle down the plug hole.

Refreshed, he donned his luxurious full-length bathrobe, bought and then embellished with the family crest at The Beverly Hills Hotel in California, a regular place to entertain clients on the West Coast. As he hacked at a block of ice with an elaborate ice pick, Sebastian recalled his star of many enjoyable dreams, Sharon Stone, and her most famous film role. He likened her feelings towards men in her character's life to his for his father at that moment. They would pass but it made him feel better. The ice covered with a generous pouring of gin followed by tonic, he slumped into a sofa and let his mind drift, while being soothed by the comforting flavours of his drink. It drifted straight to Anna.

The high-pitched ring of Anna's mobile shattered the silence in the sitting room where she had been taking a cat nap after a long walk down by the lake at Talloires. She sleepily put the phone to her ear and closed her eyes again. 'Hello?'

'Hi Anna, it's Seb.'

'Seb, hi. Nice to hear from you again so soon.'

'Well, we were rather interrupted before, so I thought I'd give you a bell to see what you're up to.' Sebastian hoped he was concealing his nerves from his voice.

'Nothing too exciting really, just walking lots and exploring. Still getting used to the mountain air. Keep dozing off!'

There was a pause then Sebastian decided *no guts no glory*. 'Anna, I've had an idea,' he said, letting the words hang for a second before adding, 'Just a mad thought, you know me!'

'Ha! Not sure I like the sound of this. I know you too well!'

After taking a deep breath and with a mindful *here goes nothing*, Sebastian took his leap of faith.

'How about a house guest for a few days?' His heart thumped. It was only a second or two before Anna responded but time was passing so slowly in his state, that to Sebastian it felt like an eternity.

'Oh! Well, I don't see why not. When were you thinking?'

Sebastian swallowed his euphoric *Yes!* and said evenly, 'Was hoping for next week.'

'That sounds fine. Gives me time to settle in properly. Let me know a day and timings when you're set. I look forward to it.'

Sebastian had been going to talk about visiting Chamonix. He had his motives but felt he had achieved enough for now and would keep that under wraps until the timing was perfect.

Upon ending the call, he felt a sense of exhilaration he normally only got from closing a top dollar deal. But this was far better than any of those, even the ones that brought a rare smile to his father's business face. A father who since Sebastian was a child, had instilled in him that life was a game of chance. Anna would be the ultimate prize.

Anna lay back slowly onto the couch. *What on earth had possessed her to agree so readily without even thinking it through? Oh, what the hell? It was done now.* She still felt a faint smattering of unease about him staying, but a sense of anticipation started somewhere deep inside her. Maybe it might help her in the long run.

The ringing of her phone once again disturbed Anna's nap. A brief moment of irritation quickly evaporated when she answered to hear Eleanor say, 'Anna?'

'Eleanor! Gosh, how lovely to hear from you!'

'How are you, dear? Enjoying your sabbatical? Sorry, not 'enjoy' exactly...'

'Yes, I am, Eleanor, in a quiet way, but it is breathtaking here and I love it. How are you?'

'Fine, dear, and thank you for asking. Well, I'm pleased you're ok. If you need anything or just want a chat, don't hesitate to call me, will you?'

Anna caught something in Eleanor's voice but dismissed it. Perhaps if she knew Sebastian was popping over to see her, Eleanor might be reassured.

'Oh, forgot to say, Eleanor, Sebastian is coming here next week. It'll be good to catch up with him after all this time.'

Anna heard the sharp intake of breath.

'Eleanor? Are you all right? What's the matter?'

'I think that will be a very good thing for both of you, dear. Do take care of yourself, won't you? I'll be thinking of you and remember, call me if you want to. Any time.' With that, they said their goodbyes.

Eleanor felt the breath rush out of her. A man and a woman... Michael's words rampaged through her head, burning a trail behind them. Please God! Not Anna and Sebastian! She would have to say something but what? How could she even begin to find the words? She picked up the phone to call Anna back but slowly replaced the receiver. Let it go for now but for how long was the dilemma. She went over everything Michael had said, again and again. It didn't make any sense. How could the man and the woman be Anna and Sebastian? It was ridiculous. Perhaps she should never have gone to Renata's clairvoyant. Blaming a cruel God for the loss of her son hadn't helped her so she had turned to the occult to find solace. Now unsure what to believe, Eleanor returned to her faith and said an earnest prayer. Something she hadn't done since Max had died.

Anna turned her mobile off and put it down on the coffee table. Enough calls! She hadn't eaten since breakfast and was ravenous. Soon, she found herself at Le Cantonnier, sipping wine and waiting for her order of *tartiflette*. She loved the deeply rich and utterly delicious dish of the region. All those potatoes, lardons, onion and lashings of Savoyard Reblochon cheese. She thought about her two phone calls. Both out of the blue, one after the other, *how odd*.

As Anna tucked into her *tartiflette*, her mobile phone which she had purposely left behind in the house, flew off the coffee table and hit the floor with a resonant crack.

CHAPTER THIRTEEN

Some time ago, in Paris

Solange quietly observed the diversity of the customers around her as she always did, out on the pavement in front of a bijou café while she waited for Marc to arrive, a simple black coffee on the ornate glass-topped table at which she sat. The midday sun was uncomfortable on her legs, so she turned them to the shade, crossing her ankles to the side in an elegant pose. It was not an entirely fraudulent air she created about her. Solange had once lived a life full of refinement and poise. Her svelte, lithe body, endless delicately muscular legs and the way she still dressed and conducted herself, all belied the truth of her present existence.

For existence it was now, except for the small hidden addition that kept her rooted to the bounds of respectability some of the time. Some raised voices from a table nearby caught her attention. There had been much unrest among the academic society and there had been many violent riots. Now a truce had been declared but how long before they again found fault with the government? The lively discussion beside her told its own story.

Solange looked out from the café terrace on Rue de la Bucherie, situated in the Latin Quarter. From there, across the river Seine, the gothic spires of Notre Dame rose up against the skyline. In bygone days, all distances from the capital city of Paris to every part of France were measured from the central point of the Place du Parvis Notre Dame, a paved square in front of the fabled cathedral. The artist in Solange always admired the timeless grace and majesty of the structure and with an inward smile, considered whether there was perhaps some parallel between Victor Hugo's tragic tale of Esmeralda and her own pathetic life thus far. However, unlike for Esmeralda, there was a light flickering brightly in Solange's life, requiring her constant effort to keep safe, maintained and nurtured. That illumination had brought her here today. She checked the time. Marc was late which was unusual. Maybe he had sensed this would not be a happy meeting.

Normally when they met for lunch, the time would be filled with silly talk and affectionate touching. She had good reason for always choosing this café, as it was a fair distance from where he lived with his parents. Marc was a promising student of accountancy. He was also Jewish. Solange was not, and certainly now, the type of woman his community would vehemently shun. They had met by chance in Square St Jean XXIII, a delightful small park behind Notre Dame, both there to catch sight of the kestrels nesting on the high ledges. There was an instant attraction and soon, they had started their futureless relationship. Solange adored Marc's unfettered life, his enthusiasm for it and the greater world in general. She had allowed their unison to continue upon the sands of her lies but, as with the shifting of sand upon rippled dunes, blown by hot desert winds, time had moved her to a place where she now had no choice but to part from her *petit ami*.

She knew her sensitive and adoring Marc would temporarily be destroyed. She understood well the pain he would suffer. Her need to break free was becoming urgent and she was sure in time he would recover, eventually setting her memory aside and finding love once more. For in truth, she knew there would have come a time when his bright future and family commitments would have demanded he part from Solange. Especially when he found out who she really was and as far from being a candidate for Marc to wed as it was possible to be.

He arrived and stood catching his breath, having run the last part of his journey from the nearest Metro stop. As usual, he handed Solange a single white rose, her favourite bloom and they kissed.

'Solange, mon amour, desolé. The tutorial ended late.'

'De rien, Marc.'

While he placed his books on the table and beckoned a waiter, Solange took in the scent of the rose and then placed it on top of the books. The waiter took the order without a word, just a firm nod of his head, very Parisian, and left them alone. Marc took Solange's hand and pressed it against his face, looking longingly into her eyes.

'I have missed you, sweet lady,' he said, then kissed her hand and placed it back on his face. 'So very much but my finals are soon, and I must work hard. I can only stay for a short while as I have another tutorial after lunch.'

'Do not worry yourself, my darling man, I have missed you too. Very much.'

Marc felt a change between them. He gently relinquished her hand and pulled his chair closer. 'What is it? Why do you seem different? Have I upset you?'

'No Marc, you could never do that,' Solange replied, softly stroking his arm and taking in his love for the last time. *But I am about to do exactly that to you, my love. Forgive me.*

The awful deed done, Solange returned to Montmartre with its bohemian residential streets. Tranquil by day in some areas but alive in others, full of artists, street vendors and the early morning spillage of undesirables from Montmartre's seedier zone, Pigalle. Tourists swarmed in the summer as they took in the open erotica in the boutiques and experienced the dark side of Paris. All this under the watchful gaze of the Basilique du Sacre Coeur, with its stunning series of domes overlooking the whole of the city from its elevated position.

Solange would often visit this very holy place and sit quietly in one of the chapels, asking for God's guidance and forgiveness. She did not attend confession. Her distrust of men filtered through even here and although they were the agents of the Lord, she could not bring herself to divulge her darkest secrets to the faceless hidden men of cloth. Thus, she would regularly throw herself at God's mercy alone.

As she climbed the dingy staircase to her friend's apartment, she could not shake her final image of Marc. She had left him sitting, quite stunned and silent, a look of incredulity upon his handsome face. In the end, Solange had chosen to tell him everything. Unabridged and without emotion. His initial disgust had turned to pity, which she didn't want or need but Marc couldn't fathom her refusal to let him help her. It was for the best. It would keep him from women like her in the future and let him find a suitable and lovely Jewish girl, which his family and the rabbi would approve of. Solange felt a pang of guilt. The life before him would most likely bore him to death.

A pretty young woman opened the door. Her apartment was untidy but clean, herself splattered in paint. Immediately Solange heard squeals of delight and her toddler daughter ran from the kitchen and leapt into her mother's arms. Solange thanked Nina and confirmed she would return later. Before she left, Nina said, 'Solange, I am teaching Sophie to paint. She loves it.' Then studying her friend, she added, 'Get some sleep, you look drawn.'

Chatting non-stop in her small but increasing vocabulary, Sophie effortlessly lifted her mother's spirits as they walked home. Solange had a phone call to make. It was the next step along the new road she now found herself walking.

Some twenty-three kilometres south west of Paris in Versailles, Isabelle Ducret prepared a *tarte tartin* as dessert for dinner that evening. She carefully laid rolled pastry over a dish full of richly stewed pears in a glistening caramelised glaze. When she was satisfied, Isabelle placed it in the oven. It was her husband's most loved dish and he always had the pleasure of turning it fruit side up.

As she started to clean up, the telephone rang. It was probably Maurice telling her he would be home late from his *pharmacie*. With dabs of flour still on her hands, Isabelle lifted the receiver, trying not to get the flour on it. For a moment, she was silent, listening, then she sat slowly on to the small chair by the hall table. Her free hand clasped to her chest. Solange. It had been some years since they had spoken.

His wife was unusually quiet through dinner, though she interacted with their guests perfectly well. But Maurice knew she was harbouring something. No sooner had the door closed on the quests, he sought out Isabelle in the kitchen.

'You didn't seem yourself during dinner.'

'I had a phone call today,' she said.

Maurice didn't need to ask anything else, he knew at once. It was the hope in his wife's eyes and lightness of spirit as she recounted her conversation with their daughter and only child. A stubborn independent girl, like a highly-strung thoroughbred race horse. She had danced as she would have raced, with the same fire and grace.

Isabelle had begun to weep. He put his arms around her and stroked her hair.

'Maurice, she wants us to have little Sophie. She is leaving Paris.'

'And you said?' he asked in resigned tones.

'Yes! I said yes! What else would I say? God only knows where she has been until now.' And there was the admonishment for both of them. Maurice remained silent, still holding his wife. She was right, of course.

'I know, I know,' he soothed. 'We said in the beginning. We should also count our blessings that Solange has finally seen sense. Can you cope with the little one?'

'Oh, Maurice!' Isabelle collapsed sobbing onto the floor. Maurice pulled her to him. This gift from their daughter would be the second child Isabelle had always wanted.

'Did she say where she was going?' Maurice gently asked.

'No... no, she didn't. I'm not even sure she knows but at least Sophie will be safely here with us. Perhaps we can persuade Solange to stay.'

Maurice kept his counsel. That was a hope too far.

With Sophie in the good care of Nina once again, Solange made her way to work. She walked past sex shops and dark smoky clubs. Pigalle's most famous cabaret was in the *Moulin Rouge* with its legendary windmill perched upon the roof. Now having moved far away from what customers in the days of Toulouse-Lautrec would have considered risqué, it still retained a burlesque feel but was now suitable for most tastes. The shows were elaborate and the girls, some baring their breasts because they got paid more, were adorned with microscopic glittering costumes festooned with large ostrich feathers. Dance sequences were the real deal and demanded a proper training in dance. It was the reason Solange had worked there for a while. As Sophie got older and sitters became more difficult to find, the strict hours and rehearsal calls moved her on to other venues, one of which she was reluctantly going to that evening. Without Nina, she would not be able to do this work which she detested. It was an affront to her talents and self-respect, but the money was good and it afforded them a reasonable, if not very comfortable, lifestyle. Certainly she would never be able to earn the same, working in the respectability of a clothes boutique during the day.

Solange had met Nina a year before while walking with Sophie in her pram one afternoon, enjoying the many artworks on show in the streets of Montmartre. She noticed a petite attractive woman standing at a small wooden easel, intense concentration in her large dark eyes. A stack of watercolour paintings was propped up against the lamp post beside her, one tethered to the post above them. It was this painting that grabbed Solange by the heart. In pale greys and creams on a muted pink background, two ballet dancers, male and female, intertwined their limbs in a classic fluid pose. Without thinking of the cost, Solange knew she must have the image, despite the raw emotions it had provoked. So their friendship began.

The dreaded regular beat of music brought Solange back to her present. She had arrived at the den of iniquity where she carved a living from the perversity presented to her on a nightly basis. A neon-signed dubious bar, it was also a strip club. Above it, a small hotel that rented rooms by the hour.

Pathetic drunken men cat-called the foulest of suggestions as the girls went wearily through their routines. Unlike all the other excruciating nights, Solange would enjoy this one.

It was her last.

CHAPTER FOURTEEN

Maurice smoked his father's old pipe, held lovingly over the years and smooth as silk. Sometimes in pensive mood as today, Maurice would just hold the pale wood, the feel reminding him of happy childhood days long gone.

His father had been a straightforward but compassionate man, often the mediator in family squabbles. Pragmatic and with a keen sense of humour, especially in situations that were not supposed to be funny. How Maurice needed those qualities now as he sat on a small balcony overlooking their petite townhouse garden. At the centre was a mature ornamental pear tree, which his family had planted as a memento of the liberation of Paris in 1945. From there, his thoughts turned to Isabelle and the day Solange was born, a terrible ordeal for both of them. Complications during the birth gave rise to an emergency Caesarean but although they managed to avoid giving Isabelle a hysterectomy, they were told that she would never become pregnant again.

Shocked by events, Isabelle lost all sense of her maternal feelings, so strong during the pregnancy. She suffered what would now be called postnatal depression but was diagnosed as just being in shock and tired. Caring dutifully for her baby in an almost robot-like state, she felt nothing for her daughter. After a couple of months, Maurice knew he must take action as he feared for his wife.

She seemed to be fading away, not just in weight but also her life force, hardly leaving the bedroom and just staring into space most days. She barely spoke and when she did, it was almost monosyllabic. So he made the difficult decision that she needed to have complete rest away from their baby.

One evening, when Isabelle lay in bed exhausted and pale after her efforts to feed the now-sleeping Solange, Maurice lay next to her and took the baby into his arms. He suggested she could benefit from having a relative, perhaps her mother, care for the baby for a few weeks. The sudden horror on his wife's face as she looked as if he had gone mad, then her desperate look at her daughter snuggled in her father's arms, was enough to tell Maurice there would be no need. He had finally found a way to get through to Isabelle and from that moment, she became the perfect, adoring, doting mother he had always hoped she could be.

Solange grew into a vivacious, pretty child who loved to dance, taking ballet lessons at her school. There was an impression of the wild and free about her and when she was eleven, her parents enrolled her into a ballet school at which she could study ballet alongside the academia. There, she shone among her peers and at sixteen, auditioned for the National Opera and Ballet in Paris. Ballet in France had been rather apathetic for many years, considered something only for the rich. Then the emergence of Roland Petit in the late 1940s revived the spirit for ballet and it began to regain its popularity.

Having won her place, to the uncontained pride of her parents, Solange began to live her dream of becoming France's prima ballerina.

Two years later that dream was abandoned forever.

Before the bell sounded, Isabelle called excitedly from the sitting room window, 'She's here!'

Maurice took a moment to collect his thoughts and then emptied the sweet pungent tobacco from the pipe, tapping it several times. He heard his wife open the door and he took a long, deep breath, preparing himself. How would his daughter be, how he remembered her? Graceful and captivating. Pregnant and desperate. Little Sophie, she must have grown so much. Would she be a beauty like her mother? Maurice became abruptly insecure in his capacity to be a good father in this moment that had unexpectedly presented itself. In business, he feared nothing and no one, his daughter was a different matter.

Mother, daughter and grandchild stood in an emotional embrace. From the shadows of the hallway, Maurice watched. Suppressed regrets welled up from within his inner self and caught in his throat, restricting it. He gulped down an involuntary sob. How could he have been so cruel? Not only to his daughter but also his cherished wife?

Solange was virtually unchanged. She retained her natural refinement and still dressed in her simple code of black. It comforted Maurice, though he also noticed an air of fatigue and resignation as he approached her. Solange looked from her mother to her father and smiled, that enchanting smile he remembered, but in her eyes was fear. He fought to keep tears at bay, the gnarled hand of guilt with its crooked fingers snatching at his soul as he finally enclosed his arms around his daughter and grandchild.

Sophie cuddled into Solange, a mildly wary look on her exquisite doll-like features. Of course, she had never met these people who seemed to have upset her mother. Any tears to Sophie represented unhappiness, that these were tears of joy and relief she would learn in years to come.

Isabelle gently stroked her grandchild's face, cooing soft words to gain her trust. She observed in detail the contours of her face and the undeniable likeness about Sophie's eyes.

Nikolai.

Maurice led them into the kitchen, their usual gathering place. Isabelle watched father with daughter and his fussing over Sophie, just as he had Solange all those years ago. For a wonderful moment, one she would hold in her soul for all time, it was as if they had never been apart.

Having studied hard, worked her body beyond its limits, Solange had finally made her first appearance on the grand stage of the Opera, as one of the many swans in the famous ballet. Her world was complete.

Visiting from the USSR was their national ballet company, world-renowned for their innovative choreography during the nineteenth century, stealing from France some of its greatest talent. The visitors would give several public performances but also take classes with the best that France had to offer. That included Solange.

During their first gathering, she was entranced by the pure skills of the Russian dancers. So much strength and balance were startling but to acquire their technical talents, the regime was brutal. Irreparable injuries to young bodies were frequent, meaning they were cast aside by the company with bleak futures outside its protection. Within this breath-taking troop was a charismatic young star called Nikolai, destined for adoration across the world. Solange found it hard to disguise her fascination with him, while, unbeknown to her, he had also privately taken note of the ballerina who had caught his eye more than once. She was aghast when he chose her for a *pas de deux* but the professional training helped her appear thankful, if a little nonchalant. Nikolai admired that. He sensed passion and strong will, a fellow non-conformist spirit and of course, her ethereal beauty.

Initially terrified she would be unable to complement his technique, Solange soon relaxed with his gentle instruction and unusual patience, so at odds with the neurotic shouting and gesticulations from her own ballet mistresses. He encouraged a freedom of her movements, previously missing, and the first touch of his hands upon her body had catapulted her into a realm of physical sensations never before experienced.

It seemed she had done well, and she received much praise from the others, whereas Nikolai said nothing. During a break, while Solange sat with her friends who excitedly asked what it had been like, he approached and asked her to sit with him to discuss his views on her performance. His Russian accent was strong, and his formation of French words was uneasy to follow but she understood well enough.

In a quiet corner, while Solange listened intently, he didn't give a critique of their brief dance together but instead spoke in a hushed voice of his wonder of life in the free world. Taught since a child of its decadence and selfish purpose, it sounded like paradise to this young vibrant Russian. Solange knew not to ask about his life, the men guarding the door to the practice room told her everything she needed to know.

For Nikolai, there was an essential element to his craft that so far had eluded him. To become unassailable worldwide and in turn, hopefully be given the ultimate chance to secure the future he had always very secretly sought. An encounter he had yet to fulfil.

At the end of the day, Solange was told that Nikolai had requested her company after everyone had left, to continue his instruction. She would be quite safe, as the sinister men that stood outside the door would remain and the Opera principals had been given every assurance. Solange was encouraged to accept as it was hoped the Russian ballet might include her in a forthcoming performance in Paris. It would be an accolade beyond their imagination.

Once alone, Nikolai led her to the centre of the room and then started the same music that was played for them earlier, but the routine he wanted to explore with her was far more intimate. He was careful to appear detached while expertly increasing the eroticism, caressing Solange as she arched and swirled in his hold. She could feel his hands on her and instinctively knew they were touching her differently. Nikolai sensed the change in her demeanour and like an orca whale engaging a young seal, cunningly manoeuvring and wearing it down, he went in for the kill.

Upon stopping their dance sequence, he changed the music to a much longer piece for the benefit of his chaperones outside, then with all the infinite grace of the *danseur* that he was, he lifted his chosen *danseuse* into his arms and took her into a small, windowless room, strewn with ballet items and a threadbare chaise-longue. He placed Solange carefully onto it, looking into her eyes. He saw no questions in them.

Solange let him caress and kiss her. There had been brief kisses with young men before but nothing of the nature she was now experiencing. He slowly began to undress her and she let him, mesmerised by his attentions, indulging in the sensuality of them and the urgent feelings they had awoken in her. The racing of her blood pounded in her ears as he suddenly held her face with one hand and tilted it back slightly, searching it. Something was released within Solange and she pulled him to her and wrapped herself around his fantastic body, moving in rhythm with him. This excited the Russian even more as he luxuriated in her untouched perfect body, kissing, licking, softly biting, then once again, he was looking into her eyes and Solange wandered through his intense gaze.

This is no tawdry Russian whore, he thought. *I could have had as many of those as I wanted but this divine creature was worth the wait.* Unlike any of the ballerinas in his homeland that threw themselves at him constantly, all attractive, some even beautiful, their downfall was their lack of self-respect and cold calculating hearts. No, they did not deserve this moment with him, this special encounter he had saved himself for. Now he was with the one he had searched for and he must treat her with care and affection.

'What is it?' Solange whispered.

Nikolai kissed her softly and said, 'Are you sure?'

'Yes, I am sure,' she replied and for the first time reached down to him, prompting a sonorous moan from Nikolai who then sought her mouth with a ferocious, almost pleading kiss as he felt for her, entered and finally added that elusive experience to his artistry, so essential for achieving his greatest wish.

In the safety of their walled garden, Sophie toddled about, sometimes chancing a run on the cool soft grass and then falling. She never cried, just picked herself up, knees and hands green and carried on with her games.

'She is so like you, Solange,' Isabelle broke the silence as the three of them watched Sophie. Then she looked at her own daughter. Her beauty had not diminished but she seemed a little older than her age. There was a reserve emanating from Solange now, and Isabelle suspected their daughter had probably not told them everything about the last few years, perhaps manipulating the truth into something more palatable for her parents.

Her plans to persuade Solange to remain with them in Versailles had been short-lived. A destination was not mentioned and both Isabelle and Maurice knew not to pry. With this renewed contact, they would tread most carefully. They would be loving guardians of Sophie for however long they were required to be and there was no indication of just what length of time that might become.

With suitable reverence, Solange said her goodbyes the following morning. She would never be able to recompense her parents for what they were agreeing to do for her. Standing on the porch of their imposing house with its tall shuttered windows, Solange forced herself to remain composed for the sake of her daughter. Battling with churning emotions, she could not let Sophie see the utter wretchedness of this moment. For her part, Sophie was quiet, watching her mother from Isabelle's arms. It was as though somehow, she instinctively knew the awful truth.

After poignant embraces, Solange turned and made her way down the stone steps to the gate. Her eyes flooded with the tears she so desperately wanted to hide. She briefly looked back toward the three figures at the door then, tears uncontrollably tumbling down her face, briskly walked away down the elegant tree-lined avenue and out of their lives.

CHAPTER FIFTEEN

As the sun's rays peered over the flat craggy peak of La Tournette, they announced an impeccable sunrise to begin another day in Talloires, bringing to life the beauty of his special realm and a crescendo of bird song.

Armand could only watch and remember how it was before and understand how it was now. To him, it was the same. Nothing had changed. Everything in its place, even Sophie. But something was different, and he was unsettled in his quiet place. A blackbird, perched on the fir tree, sang his lovely morning melody. Armand admired him, so strong and yet so fragile, like Sophie. He must protect her from harm this time, his failure before and his subsequent profanation had got him this purgatory. A place where his soul was suspended in unbearable confinement. To this diabolical place had come a voice, calling him. Armand wanted to run from the words that drew him from here. He would never leave.

Then she was there again, standing before him as she looked up to the harmonious singing above them both. Of course, he heard nothing and Armand wanted to weep. Her lovely face was serene, undisturbed and he knew his warning had gone unnoticed.

She had heard blackbird song before but somehow here, in this striking tranquil place, the notes sounded sweeter, more significant. He was superb, glossy feathers, a bright mustard yellow beak and shining black eyes that watched her as he cocked his head. Listening to her little chorister, Anna felt peaceful, grateful for the gift nature had granted her.

Then the perfume from the fir tree seemed to intensify, taking on a heady quality and Anna suddenly felt unnerved, as though a cold chiffon scarf had been brushed over her skin. She moved back from the tree and the feeling passed. Anna thought back to the phantom footsteps on the terrace and finding her phone on the floor. *Oh, that's just silly!* she remonstrated with herself. *I probably heard a bird on the roof and accidentally knocked the phone off the table.*

All the better for Sebastian arriving the next day. In the meantime, an overdue chat with her mum would alleviate her current uncomfortable aura.

Ken and Joyce were just finishing a late, leisurely breakfast when the home phone rang. Penny's ears pricked up and she turned her head toward the high-pitched ringing.

'I'll go,' Ken said, putting down the *Independent* and taking a quick swig of his tea, strong, a splash of milk and no sugar. As he went to answer the call, Joyce broke off a piece of her buttered toast and an eager mouth under the table took it gently. Ken returned to the table and said, 'It's Anna, darling,' handing Joyce the phone. 'She wants to talk to her mum.' Joyce took the phone and left the conservatory for the kitchen. Ken resumed scanning his preferred broadsheet. Penny did a one eighty under the table, as he put marmalade on his toast.

'Hello, darling, are you all right?'

'I'm fine, Mum, just felt like a chat, feeling lonely today.'

'Then why don't you come home? Be with us for the rest of your time off.' Joyce could but hope.

'Oh, Mum, I knew you'd say that! No, not yet, just wanted to catch up like we normally do. How's my Pen?'

'Normal, you know, can't put a cup of tea down where she can get at it!'

'Ha ha, yes I know!' Anna smiled, recollecting reaching for many empty cups beside the bed.

Joyce couldn't hold it back any longer. 'Anna, darling, did Sebastian call you?'

Ah! Now Anna knew who had given him her number. 'Yes, Mum, thanks. I know he's not your favourite person!'

'Oh, I'm just a funny old bird, darling, but he's been your friend for so long, I couldn't see the harm.' That was not exactly the truth, but Joyce would stay schtum for now.

Anna sensed that telling her mother he was actually coming down to see her might be better withheld for the time being. She never understood why Joyce had reservations about Sebastian. He wasn't a pompous arse with an air of superiority, like many in his high society circles and she thought he had always got along very well with her parents, being a stalwart chum to Max since childhood. It did occur to her that, since Max had died, her parents hadn't often asked about Seb. She decided not to dwell on it, to preserve the emotional healing that was already taking effect in this place.

Anna very much agreed with Estelle, it did possess a magical quality.

After the usual 'I love you's' said several times to each other before a final goodbye, it was time for her daily trek up on the higher paths above the village. Today, Anna thought, let's make it a proper route march, a military term for a walk at double time she had learned from both Max and Sebastian, who had joined the Army and Air Force Cadets respectively.

Les Dents de Lanfon towered above her in a crystal-clear sky as she kept to a fairly rapid pace up to where she could view the scenery across the lake. From her own studies during geography lessons, Anna believed the imposing hulk was an ancient volcanic plug, the strength of its substance defying the eroding of the less residual rock surrounding it through time, standing boastful above the land below. 'Look at me,' it oozed. A shadow passed over Anna and she stopped to glance up, finding a huge bird of prey circling not far above. Its head was lowered, scouring the land with intimidating pin point accurate eyes, and Anna could even see the long rapier curve at the tip of its considerable beak. The bird dipped and rose on broad static wings. She watched it with an additional, rather unwelcome image of Hannibal Lecter and knew whatever this magnificent animal chose for its next engagement, the poor creature was as good as dead already.

A vindictive stab at the back of her heels made Anna wince as she started to move again, and she realised her pace had been too fast in the heat. Two large blisters were in the making and tempered her stride on the way back to the house. Perspiration dribbled down the middle of her back and chest but goodness, she felt so alive. Through laboured breaths now, Anna inhaled the extraordinary sensations that surrounded her, deep into her lungs, holding them there and letting them fill her with a new consciousness and way of being.

Marie Boniface straightened from reseating her bean poles. The line of perfect cane tepees had been buffeted by a vicious alpine wind which occasionally came from nowhere on summer afternoons, gusting its way down through the lake valley from the south, taking many unsuspecting tourists by surprise, particularly those out on hired motor boats, who received a harsh impromptu lesson in how to steer into the suddenly choppy waters that had been pristine and calm.

Marie stood, two placating hands pressed against her lumbar region as she noticed the English woman walking to the house with a very faint limp. Since their brief meeting, having spoken to Father Luc and been counselled by the family, she found that those fierce deep-seated feelings toward her had lessened, though not evaporated completely.

How can two women look so alike? she thought. Was it really just an incomprehensible coincidence? If so, as Josephine had said, then it was a damned spiteful one. Marie found herself once again returning to her very exclusive introspections about Sophie.

God had sent her precious son a much prayed for bride and she, Marie, had not trusted in His judgement, treating Sophie with barely hidden contempt. Perhaps this twist of fate was His doing as a punishment. Repent and be forgiven, that was the teachings of her church. It seemed perhaps she must make peace with this *anglaise* and there was an idea brewing.

Each August, the Boniface family threw a fête for their fellow villagers in Perroix, always held at the rambling farmhouse under huge awnings stretched across the courtyard. Classic long tables sat side by side on the worn cobbles, wine and beer flowing endlessly. The women of Perroix made the copious amounts of food, traditional rustic fare.

This year, Marie would break with tradition and village lore and invite an outsider, *l'anglaise,* and hoped He would take notice.

It took every ounce of will power to command her feet to climb the steps to the terrace, the sharp pain from the blisters excruciating now. Anna sat on the top step and gingerly removed her trainers, there were two bloody holes in her heels. Then suddenly she swung round, sure somebody had been standing behind her. She looked about the empty terrace and frowned. Shaking her head, she went to open the front door thinking just how timely Sebastian's visit was, considering these seemingly increasing blips in her sobriety.

As he watched her on the terrace, his hands balled into white knuckle fists and a darkness pervading his face, Armand felt a blazing seething rage.

CHAPTER SIXTEEN

His Mercedes-AMG GT Roadster ate the early morning autoroute like his idol Lewis Hamilton's Mercedes race car demolished an F1 circuit. The glistening silver-grey curves resembled that of a stalking lioness, poised for attack, her legs replaced with super low-profile alloy wheels.

A Ministry of Sound CD blasted out through the Burmester surround sound system, a hypnotic 'house' throb thumped around the personalised leather interior. His car was a statement. It said *Fuck you*.

Sebastian had taken a detour from the route out of Calais and driven to Reims to pick up a case of champagne from his preferred house of Krug. His most formidable challenge lay ahead and everything had to be presented perfectly. Only the very best would do, which was why he had also made a dinner reservation for that evening at L'Hotel Imperial in Annecy for the best start possible. He had wined and dined countless very precious young socialites into his bed but Anna was his most coveted prize. She would require a careful, slow and considered development, expertise and oh yes, he was a hundred percent prepared for it.

Eleanor gazed out through the window of her sanctum. Husband Alistair was asleep on a sun lounger on their large York Stone patio, leading out onto an almost golfing green quality lawn. It certainly helped Alistair with his putting practice. She took a long draw on her cigarette, feeling unusually relaxed. It had been a while. She nearly jumped out the chair when her mobile rang on the window sill. *Silly cow,* she mused and said, 'Hello?'

'Is this Eleanor?'

'Michael?'

'Hello, lovey, sorry to call you out of the blue.'

Eleanor sat up straight and took a quick, silent drag of much-needed calming nicotine. Why on earth was he calling her? Before she could enquire, Michael continued, 'Sorry to drop this on you but could we possibly meet today?'

'I... I think so,' Eleanor said looking at her watch on a shaky wrist. 'What time?'

'As soon as you can, really,' Michael replied, trying not to project the mild panic rising in him.

'Whatever's wrong, Michael?' Eleanor suddenly felt chilled.

'I just need to see you, lovey.'

'Four thirty?'

'Perfect.'

Anna sat on the terrace, perusing the garden and the luminous fir tree. It seemed to glow, exuding that sweet pine scent that had enveloped her before. She got up and walked over to the tree and as she got close, two strong protective arms encircled her waist and she turned within them.

Facing him, his eyes immersed in hers and watery with tears, his stare seemed to bore into her soul. She could hardly breathe and terror rose up inside her. Anna screamed but no sound would come. Breaking from his ever-tightening grip, she ran for the house, but he followed and was almost upon her again. The door wouldn't open as she frantically wrestled with the large black iron handle, as it kept slipping from her grasp.

'No!' Anna finally cried out and sat up in bed. It took several seconds before she regained her composure through gulping breaths. Shivering, she pulled the duvet up over her head and wept. The same dream, over and over again, but this had been graphic and so utterly real, this time she could recall every awful detail and that was why she shivered.

The man wasn't Max.

'Hi Anna, it's Seb. You ok? You don't sound yourself.'

'Seb! Great to hear from you!' She really meant it at that moment. 'Just woken up actually, had a bit of a bad dream, that's all.' Anna realised she must have sounded like a little girl and regretted what she had said.

'Too much of that luscious French cheese before bedtime!' Sebastian laughed. 'Well, I'm just outside Chalon-sur-Saone, north of Mâcon, so not long now.'

'Drive carefully, Seb.'

'Anna, darling, you're not my mother!'

Call ended, Anna was more enthusiastic for his visit than ever before. Recalling Estelle's words again, *magical* was not quite the description she would have chosen that morning. Just who was that man? Apparently desperate in some odd, nightmarish way. Such questions would have to wait because the house required making ready for Sebastian's arrival. She hoped he was true to his old form, they would have so much fun.

Michael opened the door. 'Come in, lovey.'

'What's happened, Michael? I'm so worried.'

Walking her through to the now familiar room, he said, 'I know, I'm so sorry but honestly, I've not experienced this before.'

Eleanor stopped and looked at Michael as he sat in the normal place on his sofa. 'Experienced?'

'Lovey, just come in and sit down for me. I'll tell you everything. Oh, look at me being so rude, would you like some tea?' He hadn't been himself for several days.

'No, thank you, Michael.'

'Then I'll begin. It's the woman with the baby. Seems she can push her way through all the others. I've not been able to function properly, cancelling readings left, right and centre. As far as I know, there has only ever been one other case like this.'

Eleanor was still, her spooked insides turning into soup. 'Another "case"?' she managed in a strained voice.

'Let me explain,' Michael answered.

Anna heard Sebastian's car pull to a crunching halt on the gravel driveway. He revved the engine, the sound deep and throaty, to tell her he was finally there.

SO Sebastian! she mused. A quick check in the mirror and she went out to welcome him. He stood by the car with a ridiculously huge bouquet of flowers and smiled that irresistible slayer smile he was known for.

'Hello, you gorgeous creature,' Sebastian said, his usual greeting for her, placing the bouquet on top of the roof of the car. Anna was unexpectedly filled with a rush of choking emotion. Running to hug him, she threw her arms around his neck and gave him a firm kiss on the cheek.

'Anna, darling, are you ok?' he said into her luxurious hair, inhaling its newly-washed perfume. She finally pulled apart from him with a sniffle, looking coy and extremely embarrassed. 'You are a Narna, Anna!' They both laughed and hugged again. He handed her the bouquet and opened the boot of the car. 'Can you be ready for supper in ten?' he asked, picking up the case of Krug.

'Ten what?' Anna asked with an impish grin.

'Minutes, darling, minutes! Got a reservation and we should just make it in time if we leave quickly.'

'Where?' Anna enquired.

'You probably don't know of it but the Hotel Imperial in Annecy. It's right on the lake.'

She did know it and couldn't wait. 'I'll be five minutes,' she said and ran into the house.

Sebastian slowly walked up to the terrace and put down the champagne, returning to his car to fetch his bags. Oh, this was going better than he could have expected but he remembered he had striven to make changes about himself. He needed to heed those and if successful, he would be closer to making Anna his own.

Seated in the restaurant, she looked out to the lake, a dark mill pond. Further out towards Sevrier, just south of Annecy on the western bank, the moon's light danced upon the ebony water. A chime of a bottle being taken from a solid silver ice bucket and Sebastian dismissing the sommelier, reeled Anna back into the room.

Before popping the cork, he said, 'Make a wish.' Anna was so overwhelmed, she couldn't think of a single thing to wish for and smiled with a shy shrug. 'Well, I've made one,' he said and deftly held the bottle with finger and thumb on the base as he poured the frothy liquid into their glasses without spilling a drop, turned the bottle to prevent drips and placed it in the bucket, covering it with a starched white napkin. They clinked glasses and sipped vintage Veuve Cliquot. 'Thirsty work driving here!' It hadn't been, but he had a sudden, unanticipated attack of nerves.

Anna looked surprised and said, 'Gosh, heathen!'

'Actually, I'm a bit on edge, darling, first meeting since the... the... um...'

'Funeral,' Anna finished. 'It's passed, Seb, this is now, let's drink to that.'

Sebastian topped up Anna's glass and poured himself another. They toasted to 'now' and he called over the waiter and ordered. Anna let Seb, a consummate fine dining maestro, make the choices. Lobster Thermidor to begin, chateaubriand to follow and crêpes suzette, prepared in a flaming pan at the table, to finish. It couldn't have been a more perfect menu for her, he had remembered well.

They arrived back at the house just after midnight.

'Sorry, Cinders, not quite before the final stroke of the clock but I think "pumpkin" suits you!'

'Oh, very droll, Seb,' Anna responded, then realised she had missed his silly humour. The longing for Max to also be with them as before was unbearable. 'Thank you for a lovely evening, totally unnecessary but gratefully received, kind sir.' She did a theatrical swashbuckling bow.

'A nightcap before bed?' Sebastian asked as they entered the house.

'I'm fit to drop, Seb. Sorry.'

'Don't worry, you sleep well, princess.'

She bid him goodnight and closed the sitting room door. He unzipped a bag and opened a bottle of Scotch. He went out onto the terrace and sat looking up at the amazing night sky, the air so fine and clear he could see the band of the Milky Way. It was apparent he had been right all along, watching and admiring in the shadow of his old school friend, silent in his need. Anna was everything he had ever wanted in a woman, but could he make himself her man?

CHAPTER SEVENTEEN

Eleanor drove to the park that enhanced an otherwise dull part of Hampstead, its large handsome mansion houses blemished with the manic security measures of their occupants, and of course, the mandatory satellite dishes. There used to be a comforting communal atmosphere not too many years ago but now, apart from the bustling high street, you barely saw a soul. The immaculate gardens were conveniently located close to her house and having parked, Eleanor lit a cigarette. After blowing the first lungful out of the window, she picked a speck of tobacco from her lower lip, not very ladylike but hell, right now she just didn't care.

Eventually she got out of her car and walked under a canopy of heavily foliated trees, a random leaf falling in the increasing breeze. She found her special bench and sat at the centre of it, hoping it might deter anyone joining her on it. She required total solitude to dissect and evaluate what had been said during her meeting with Michael.

The silence as Michael drifted into his dreamlike condition, had an unearthly fragility. Eleanor had concentrated on keeping her breathing quiet, not wanting to cause any disturbance in his vibes, or whatever they were. He held her necklace again and sometimes strands of meagre light from small gaps in the drawn velvet curtains, gave rise to momentary glints of gold, bright little flashes in the sombre surroundings. Eleanor wondered if they were an indication the spirits were present and felt a wave of cold roll over her.

'There is a house.' Michael's sudden statement made her jump. Again. 'It was their home but now there is so much regret and tremendous anger.' Michael's eyes were closed, his head bent forward, the necklace held in both hands over his knees. There was an eerie pause, then he spoke again. 'This woman and child have come back from the other side to help her husband reach the light. He keeps himself away from it. There is someone holding him there.'

Eleanor's skin crawled and she was close to crying out. *Come ON!* She checked herself.

'There is a woman to whom he is now drawn. There is a man with the woman. It is why he resists the light.' With that, Michael nodded his head, straightened up and opened his eyes, looking directly at Eleanor. 'I think I understand now.'

She sat fixed and unable to speak. *Understand what?* she asked herself. Michael stood up and opened the curtains. Warm light flooded into the room, but it was still icy cold. He held out his hand and Eleanor took it like a frightened child. 'I think we both need some tea or maybe something stronger!' Michael led her to the kitchen.

Two pigeons pecked around her feet, heads bobbing as they cooed at each other, the iridescent purples and greens of their neck feathers caught in the evening sunlight. Eleanor watched, and tried to find her way through the details.

According to Michael, the mysterious spirit was of a woman who had died before her husband. He was now also dead but remained earthbound. Recently there had been an event that weakened his ability to hide from those that were there to help him pass over successfully.

To say this had been a bit bewildering was a total understatement and if she were honest, too farfetched to comprehend. Yet, why did it all seem to make so much sense to her? Like a missing piece of a jigsaw being found and completing a picture, such as the ones in her dreams. Eleanor was quite certain that Michael's spirit and the woman she kept seeing standing on the banks of a body of water, were one and the same. It felt right. The compelling urge to see a clairvoyant in the first place seemed to have been merely a scene within a play, another act now unfolding before her.

Anna and Sebastian. A man and a woman. Was she just putting two and two together and making five? It really could all be just a stupid coincidence and Michael an accomplished fraud. The heaviness in her chest told Eleanor that this was all very real.

Sebastian was in his bathrobe, sipping freshly-made coffee and concentrating totally on his laptop screen, his fingers moving quickly across the keys. For him, the family business was 24/7 and even in the midst of his present personal task, there was always a window to keep his head up and communicate whenever he could, particularly with his father who had sent him a bank of information to examine and get back with opinions and suggestions. Sebastian knew he would need to action this immediately, markets and not least his father ran at a breakneck speed.

The door opened, and Anna walked in, wearing just her shorty night shirt. Horrified to see Sebastian already up, she quickly closed the door and ran back upstairs to attire herself more moderately. He was so engrossed in the figures before him, Sebastian didn't notice.

Wearing jeans and T-shirt, Anna returned.

'Morning! Didn't expect you up so early! Do I smell coffee?'

'Morning, gorgeous. Yes, get yourself a cup and join me,' he said without looking up from the screen. 'This won't take much longer.'

As Anna moved around the coffee table and sat at the other end of the sofa, she noticed his surprisingly well-pedicured feet. 'Sleep all right?' she asked.

'Mm, wonderfully, the mountain air, I suppose. I did wake up feeling a chill a couple of times, but I was just shattered,' he replied, closing his laptop. 'Sorry about this, needed to catch up with business, hope you don't mind.'

'Don't be silly, of course you have to. There's another duvet, if you want it.'

'That's ok, darling, I was just tired. Don't fuss, you're being my mother again!'

The heat had determined the day's agenda. A cooling dip in the lake and picnic at Le Plage, the 'beach' in Talloires. Not a beach as such but a beautiful lawn reaching to the lake, several sets of steps down into the lake and a pontoon anchored a few metres from them.

Once settled near the edge, Anna and Sebastian descended the steps into the cool waters of Lac Annecy. Being a freshwater lake, there is none of the buoyancy found in the sea. Anna had never been the best swimmer and had let her fitness slip in recent months, so she was grateful for a strong, helping hand from Sebastian onto the pontoon. Alone on the gently undulating platform, Sebastian lay down and stretched out to his full six foot two, hands behind his head, water glistening on his well-toned body.

Anna sat with her back to him, dangling her feet in the lake. 'Lovely, isn't it?' she said.

Sebastian lifted his head and smiled, then rested it back onto his arms. 'Yes, this is just perfect.' *Very perfect,* he thought. *Time for the next stage.* 'Anna?'

'Mm?' she responded, still watching the clear water lap over her feet.

'Have you considered a day in Chamonix?' His breath held as he waited. This was crucial.

Anna turned to him and then looked out across the water, before turning again to find his eyes focused on her own.

'I have, Seb, and yes, it makes sense.'

'It won't be easy for you but...'

'Nothing's been easy since Max died,' she interrupted. 'Nothing. I'm here to sort myself out and I can't think of a better place to go. I need to understand, to make my peace.'

Sebastian woke up with a start from a deep sleep. The darkness outside indicated a very early hour. He felt chilled again but this time he also felt a restlessness. He needed a hot drink and he pulled on a fleece. He pondered whether he was coming down with a cold, this was the usual hot summer in the Alps after all.

The bedroom door wouldn't open. He tried again, checked the door and kept pulling. It was stuck fast.

'For fuck's sake!'

Now frustrated, he yanked at it again and nearly fell back onto the bed, as the door opened with ease.

CHAPTER EIGHTEEN

They reached the Chamonix valley, imposing high mountains guiding them in. As they neared the outskirts of Chamonix, Sebastian slowed the car so Anna could look up at the permanent glacier, La Mer de Glace, to their right. The end of a massive sea of snow, ice and rock slowly chewing away at the mountains in its path. Carving a new valley as it devoured everything on a constant, indomitable journey, Sebastian's motive as precise in execution.

Some years before, Anna and Max had travelled up to this glacier, taking the rack and pinion railway, then a short cable car ride to the ice grottos. Looking at it now, she remembered, as if it were yesterday, the strange feeling she had experienced, walking amongst the ice sculptures, newly created each year. There was a disturbing sound of creaking around them as the glacier imperceptibly scraped its way down to where the warm temperatures of the summertime Chamonix valley would cause the leading edge to melt away at a faster rate each year.

Anna turned back from the spectacle and just stared ahead, saying nothing. Sebastian left his passenger to her thoughts and continued into the town. He parked near the *telepherique* station. Above them was the reason he had brought her here. The very thing that she needed to be at peace with, if he was to have any chance of successfully closing this best of all deals.

'We'll get some lunch first, shall we?' Sebastian asked, hand gently placed on Anna's shoulder. She nodded with a smile that didn't reach her eyes.

'Bit surreal being here again.'

'I know,' Sebastian said. 'In a much smaller way, it is for me too.' He had never returned and was surprised by unwelcome emotions rapidly welling up. 'Where would you like to eat?' he said, changing the subject.

'Oh, I'm not sure. You choose, I don't mind.'

They started to walk up Avenue de l'Aiguille du Midi. Sebastian held out his hand and Anna took it. After a few minutes they reached a bridge spanning the river Arve. In the early spring, after heavy rain fall, it raged milky grey as melting snow, mud and small rocks cascaded down the slopes. Now, as they crossed the bridge, it was a clear emerald trickle in comparison. Sebastian paused to look at the river. All his life, apart from Max, he had let everything of any importance drift away like the natural flotsam bobbing past on the surface of the water below. Anna might just be his last chance of real happiness in an otherwise extravagant and superficial existence.

'I know,' he said, 'I'll take you to our secret place.'

Anna lifted her gaze up from the river and raised her eyebrows. 'Secret place?'

'Because they make the best crêpes ever!'

'But why is it secret?'

'Because if we had told everyone in our motley crew, it would have spoilt it. We went there when we wanted time away from them.'

He didn't have to say his name because Anna knew Sebastian was talking about Max.

They walked along Rue du Docteur Paccard, full of bars, nightclubs and various souvenir shops.

'Are you ok, Anna?' he asked, reaching for her hand again.

'Mm,' she confirmed and without averting her eyes from exploring her surroundings, put her hand in his.

Sebastian was quiet. In fact, he seemed very sensitive toward her and she felt maybe this was a Sebastian she had never met before. Her memories of him were full of bravado, drinking competitions, a constant flow of stunning ladies from equally wealthy families. A man burning the candle at both ends and never tiring of life. Not for a moment.

This calm, collected considerate man was a bit of an enigma. Perhaps they could build a friendship as themselves, rather than what they had through their individual connections to Max. It would be comforting to keep Sebastian in her life, someone who had been so close to her husband and most likely knew him better than she ever had.

They ate the lightest, most delicious savoury crêpes in a small, almost hidden away family restaurant in the quieter western area of Chamonix town. After lunch, Seb led the way to the *telepherique* to take them up to a place he hadn't been to since March.

'I never expected to come back here,' said Anna quietly.

Seb said nothing, just reached for her hand in comfort. As they stepped into the cable car, he stumbled as, without warning, a peculiar sense of foreboding settled over him.

Half way up, they had to wait ten minutes for the second car that would take them to the top. It was an opportunity to observe hikers who start their chosen routes among the huge rocks and boulders strewn across the Plan de l'Aiguille, a small plateau where, along a well-trodden path, stood a wooden chalet selling refreshments. It also served as a waiting place for those who decided this was far enough while others, like Sebastian and Anna, who wanted the whole experience, would continue up. The views were still astonishing, even at this level.

Not for the faint-hearted, the second cable car groaned its way slowly up the mountain side. Anna clutched Seb's hand even tighter as her fear of heights began to play its usual nasty games. As they got closer to the station, the rock became sheer and the sense of being dangled over the edge of the world was all too real as the car bumped and swayed before coming to a halt at the station. Before Anna could catch her breath in the cold thin air, they were standing looking out from an opening in the rock wall of the station. Ahead of them was a bridge and the only route across to the large construction of wood and glass perched atop another sheer rock, housing restaurants, cafes and various viewing platforms. The familiar tango of pins and needles danced in her fingers and toes. *Stop being such a wuss,* she told herself, *you're perfectly safe.*

'Right!' she said with authority. 'Lead on, Macduff!'

Sebastian linked his arm through hers to give her a feeling of security, well aware of her phobia. It had driven Max to distraction in the beginning until he finally managed to get Anna to at least try. Over the years, she had even surpassed her own expectations but the phobia remained and it was just letting her know that.

With slightly wobbly legs, Anna, guided by Sebastian, advanced to the centre of the bridge and paused to look out at the unsurpassable views of peaks spread far into the distance. To their right, the dazzling summit of Mont Blanc rose up ahead of them, the ever-present winds blowing a fine mist out from the peak, its raw beauty spellbinding.

'I want to look over the edge,' said Anna, surprising even herself.

'Are you sure?

'Just hold on to me, Seb. I've not looked over it before, only outwards from it.'

So, with Sebastian's arms firmly around her waist and pulled close to him, Anna edged to the side. She paused with her eyes closed and took some deep breaths, then opened them and forced herself to look down, immediately finding the deep cracks she had come to face. The vertical ice walls of the deadly fractures glared at her with their pale, translucent blue menace. Beyond further, the darkness of hell. Somewhere not far from where she stood, just beneath one of the nearest peaks, one of these sinister breaches had become Max's hell. Her hell. An involuntary sob suddenly burst from Anna, Sebastian grabbed her shoulders, turned her round and enveloped her in his arms as she shook with desperate wails into his chest.

His own dire memories flooded through to the surface and he also choked up but checked himself and swallowed it back. The slightest show of tears quivered in his eyes. He had to be strong for this lady, she needed to feel protected and he began to realise how he might actually be quite good at it. As he held Anna while she continued to weep, he would have traded his whole frivolous life just to have been able to say there and then that he loved her.

Now recovered and very thankful to her friend for holding her tight, letting the emotions she had bottled up since Max died finally pour out of her, Anna decided to go to the highest viewing point, under a massive transmitter aerial. They looked down on to the Vallée Blanche, a treacherous white sheet where those who dared to climb up further made base camps.

'What makes them push themselves to the edge of their lives?' Anna asked into the thin mountain air. Sebastian remained silent, letting her work through her thoughts. 'I could never truly understand before but now, looking at this hypnotic magnificence with a changed perspective, I hope maybe I have some basic sense of them.'

Returned to Perroix, they sat outside Le Cantonnier sipping a local *Eau de Vie*. Anna picked up her glass and let the soft evening sunlight illuminate the caramel-coloured liquor.

'*Water of life,*' she said, not to Sebastian, more to herself. Then directed at her friend, 'What do you consider to be your 'water of life', Seb?'

'Sorry?' he said wondering what Anna meant.

'*Eau de Vie* translates to *Water of Life.*'

'Ah, of course, I see. Interesting question!' He became thoughtful. 'Hm, not sure.' His mind travelled to another time in his life. He took a sip of the *Eau de Vie* and continued. 'I once needed some time out from everyone, mainly family. You know the scenario. Well, anyway, I rented a tiny antiquated cottage in mid-Wales near a little place called Dolgellau in the foothills of Snowdonia. There was no phone signal and I was woken up by sheep at the window every morning.

'Gosh, so not you, Seb!' Anna smiled.

'I suppose.' The amusement in Anna's voice was a harsh slap across his face. She hadn't meant it but the feeling it produced was profound. Sebastian gulped down the rest of the *Eau de Vie* and resumed his recollection. 'It was up high on a hillside and there was a forest nearby. A short walk into the forest, there was this amazing waterfall. I used to go there and sit watching it. I felt so revived when I left, so I guess I could say that waterfall was *Water of Life* for me.'

When he had finished, Sebastian smiled like an embarrassed child, surprised he had opened up to Anna so willingly. Even so, he kept the reason for his venture to himself. A broken engagement and broken by him. Both families had been furious, not to mention the lady herself.

'So, *quid pro quo*, then. What's your 'water of life'?' he asked Anna, leaning closer and perusing her lovely face.

Anna was quiet for a beat then said simply, 'Love.'

CHAPTER NINETEEN

Previously, in Versailles

Sophie studied the architecture she was trying to reproduce, occasionally glancing at her work, deciding whether her final adjustments were exact. After several minutes of scrutiny, she was satisfied that the essence of the Grand Trianon, the larger of two small palaces within the grounds of the Chateau de Versailles, had been captured. She began to highlight her charcoal and pencil drawing with an artist's pen. The dark ink flowed from the hair-fine nib, transforming the scene. It was Sophie's favourite media and deliberately chosen. In times of sadness or uncertainty, the concentration and precision of such work was the perfect antidote. In her bag was a letter.

With the finished piece safe in a substantial folder, hanging from a wide strap over her shoulder, Sophie walked slowly to her favourite part of this beautiful parkland. North of the other small palace, or Petit Trianon, the gardens were less formal with winding paths she loved to stroll.

By chance quite alone in this tranquil spot, she sat on the grass next to a fragrant rose bed and took the envelope out of her bag. She had always known this letter would arrive one day, but the wait had been long and at times through the years, her motivation to continue that belief had wavered. The writing on the envelope, postmarked St Tropez, was her mother's.

Maurice and Isabelle had waited patiently for Solange to contact them after she had again vanished from their lives, this time her daughter's included. They had never expected any immediate communication or even regular contact. Neither could have envisaged she would let nearly eight years pass and materialise as a voice on the telephone.

When the infuriated Isabelle had handed the phone to Sophie after much pleading from Solange, the child regarded it curiously as her grandmother gently stroked her hair and nodded encouragement. Sophie said, 'Allo?', then just listened to the words from a vaguely familiar voice before saying 'au revoir' and handing the phone back to Isabelle. She returned to the sitting room where her friends were waiting.

After closing the door behind Sophie, Isabelle raged at her daughter. Solange let her mother rant and waited for her to finish. Finally, there was a terse pause and Solange spoke.

'I know I have no defence, Mother. I cannot explain...'

'No, you never could, could you?' Isabelle cut in. 'Your daughter deserved better!'

Solange sighed. 'Whatever you think of me, and I don't doubt I deserve everything you feel, there has never been a day when I didn't think about Sophie. I love her.'

'What is it you want, Solange?' Isabelle asked icily.

'To speak with my daughter and I have done so. Thank you for that, at least.'

'Then I suggest you stay away and let Sophie continue her life with no more of these self-centred interferences when it suits you. It serves no purpose other than to satisfy a need in you and you've always been good at that, Solange, haven't you?' There was a brief silence.

Then Solange simply said, 'I understand' and hung up.

Isabelle stood still holding the phone when the call ended. Her blood felt as though it had frozen and she began to tremble. This was her only child whom she was discarding from their lives, like a pear that had fallen from the tree and become rotten, but she felt no hesitation in doing so. Where she had been unable to with Solange, Isabelle was determined to protect Sophie. The call was never mentioned again.

Now ready to read her mother's letter, Sophie slid her thumb under the seal and carefully opened the envelope. She peered into it before gently extracting the two-page letter, like a delicate artefact being examined by an archaeologist. A quick overview revealed it was signed, *Your mother*.

Your mother, she thought. Of course, she accepted the biological fact but nothing more. Isabelle was her mother in the truest sense of the word. As for her biological father, Sophie only knew the few details her grandparents had spoken of some years before when she had finally asked. They told her he had been a promising ballet dancer in Paris but was tragically killed in a car accident, his name was Nikolai, and this was the cause of her mother's 'depression' and why she had gone away. Sophie never pressed for his surname but maybe her mother might talk of such things now.

Her memories of Solange were few. One that she would recall often was being looked after by a kindly-faced lady in a messy overall and who laughed a lot. Sophie also remembered the many paintings she would look at and make up stories about. It was then Sophie felt a pull on her heart, a feeling of gratitude to her mother for leaving her with that lady. It was where she indirectly had given Sophie a life gift, her art. It had served her well in the years since.

Having successfully graduated from the Sorbonne, she was now an accomplished artist who hoped one day to open her own gallery.

Before reading the neat handwriting in blue ink on pale grey paper, she travelled back in time to a certain telephone call and a softly well-spoken voice.

'Sophie, my darling, this is Mummy. I know this must be difficult and confusing, but I wanted to wish you a happy birthday. I have never forgotten and I have loved you always.' Solange waited for some response but none came. 'I cannot speak for long,' she said, only too aware the phone might be snatched away by Isabelle at any moment. 'But please know I leave you in the love and care of your grandparents because I can't give you the life they can.' Isabelle's muffled voice had drifted through and she knew to finish quickly before the chance was gone. 'I will write to you, my darling, I promise.'

Drawing in a long, deep breath, her heart beating a little faster, Sophie began to read the letter she had waited upon for nearly fourteen years.

Seated around the kitchen table, tucking into a bouillabaisse with toasted croutons, the omnipresent but essential baguette and red wine, Maurice, Isabelle and Sophie laughed about an incident in the market that morning. A heated row had broken out between stallholders and Isabelle play-acting them in animated fashion brought tears to her husband's eyes. He nearly choked on the aromatic fish and tomato stew. Sophie listened and interjected at times but mostly she was quiet, her thoughts elsewhere. She had to find a way to tell the two dearest people in her life that she was going away for a while and she knew the reason would distress them both.

As Isabelle concluded her dramatics, Sophie took an unladylike swig of her wine.

'Sophie!' Maurice checked her, stew dripping from his spoon suspended between bowl and mouth.

'Regardez!' she checked him back, indicating bouillabaisse was dropping into his lap.

Then it was time to drop the bomb shell.

'I received a letter today.' She had their attention immediately. Maurice looked at Isabelle and her reaction was a stony stare, meeting his questioning eyes. She knew.

'Letter?' Isabelle managed to sound level.

'I will be leaving for the south of France tomorrow,' Sophie said, looking at her grandmother. 'I'm going to see my mother,' to her grandfather's now-bewildered face.

Maurice slammed a fist onto the table, stew slopped out of their bowls and dribbled down the sides, pooling on the table mats. He grabbed at the carafe and poured a large measure of wine. He looked from his glass to Sophie as he set the carafe down with a thud and demolished his wine in one go. Isabelle just gently took Sophie's hand under the table and squeezed it gently. *Oh, dear Lord! It was happening again.*

'She is very ill,' Sophie said. 'I have to go to her, please try and understand?'

'How ill?' Maurice demanded. He knew his daughter well and wouldn't have been surprised if this was another ruse of hers, to get at Sophie. 'Well?' he asked, reaching for the carafe again. Isabelle looked at him to berate him but he ignored her.

'She is dying,' Sophie said and then ran upstairs to her room and slammed the door.

Maurice picked up his wine glass and went into the garden. Isabelle said several prayers as she cleared the table. The resonance of the silence between them was almost audible.

CHAPTER TWENTY

St Tropez. A stunning playground for the rich and famous. A spectacle adorned by a sparkling sea, surrounding the rocky peninsula upon which St Tropez sits. To the north, the Massif des Maures, a rambling mountain range stood guard over the self-absorbed glitterati. Originally a picturesque fishing village, it was engulfed by the success of a budget film called *And God Created Woman*, starring a fabulous young starlet called Brigitte Bardot. The simple heart and soul of St Tropez was forever lost amidst the descent of those who now make it their own. Even so, set apart from the other popular resorts along the Côte d'Azur, there is still the fundamental quality within its old streets and this was the setting where Sophie would meet her mother at a well-known people-watching spot, Le Café.

Solange had insisted on a prominent table on the terrace, so she could observe the crowds and hopefully catch sight of her daughter as she approached. She was a regular at this chic bar and restaurant, knowing the owner well so she was seated at the perfect table for her undertaking. Dressed tastefully in muted tones, her hair scraped back from a still-alluring face, she sipped water, as she scanned the passing crowd. Her eyes were not as bright as they once had been, and a subtle full make-up had been necessary, even in the blazing southern French sun, to conceal the doughy pallor of her chemo-ravaged skin.

Retaining the elegance of days long gone, Solange cut a charismatic presence among the other clientele. Men snatched glances as her eyes briefly met theirs while looking for her daughter, but she did not notice their flirting, it was all irrelevant to her now.

Then she found her, a tall, slender young woman walking with purpose toward the café. Solange was watching a mirror image of her once-vibrant youthful self. She stood and waved, the woman stopped and hesitatingly waved back, her beguiling face lightening with a questioning smile. Solange felt she might collapse with the intensity of the feelings rushing through her frail body. She steadied herself and absent-mindedly touched her hair and smoothed her fitted classic shift dress.

Sophie stood before her mother, who, though painfully thin, really was quite beautiful. Solange spoke first.

'Sophie. My Sophie.'

'Hello, Mother.'

The words sounded strange. Neither woman moved to embrace the other in case it was too soon. A shy atmosphere prevailed as they both sat, still regarding each other intently. Solange lifted a hand and caught the eye of a waiter. He had been waiting for the gesture and brought champagne to the table. Solange smiled and said, 'Only the best for this occasion. You are lovelier than I could ever have imagined. I am so proud you are my daughter. This is the happiest day of my life.'

'Thank you, Mother. I too believe this to be a good day,' Sophie replied as they held up their champagne, the glasses singing a pleasant note as they touched, sealing the toast.

Solange called the waiter back and ordered a light Salade Niçoise for them. Sophie watched her mother's prowess in working the restaurant and smiled. She could see her grandfather in Solange, commanding the waiting staff just as her mother was.

Solange caught Sophie watching and with a tone of modesty and a wink, said, 'Oh, please don't be impressed. I have worked in too many hotels and bars not to know how to do this!'

It was a small insight to the secret life her mother had lived, and Sophie welcomed it silently, then said, 'Mother?'

Solange had wanted to hear her daughter say that since that day in Paris. Now, being as close to death as she was, the words sounded all the sweeter.

'Why did you leave?' Sophie asked in an unassuming way. The forthright question caught Solange by surprise but she didn't show it. It pleased her that Sophie was so forward and straight. Life was easier for those with strong spirits. The time had come to say everything she had prepared for this moment, before the emotion of this bitter sweet meeting suppressed her infant courage.

'There is much to say, Sophie but first, I am so very sorry. Sorry for everything. It means little now. I only ask that one day you might forgive this stupid old woman.' Sophie watched Solange as she struggled for words. 'When I left you that day and walked away with that image of you three at the door, my heart withered in that very moment. My darling girl, I just wasn't prepared for you. I wasn't prepared for life. The things that happen you can never expect. Good things, bad things, wonderful things. I was still a child myself and there you were, a tiny human being ...' Her voice trailed off and tears spilled down her face.

'My grandparents have looked after me well, Mother. I have had a wonderful life. I still don't understand why you couldn't stay.'

'Oh, Sophie, one day you might find yourself in a situation where even with all the advice in the world from those you love, you must make a decision alone. I made the wrong decision and then, I found I couldn't go back. I was scared.'

'Scared?' Sophie asked, 'Why?'

'Of you, of my parents.' A faint cry escaped from her as tears pooled. 'I was weak, Sophie. It was that weakness that kept me from being with you and it was that weakness that stopped me coming back.'

'But you were with me for over two years. Why then go away?' The questions were not said with anger or blame, just a daughter's bafflement.

'I was, am a stubborn creature, Sophie. I wanted to prove I could cope. To show them. Hah!' Solange released a sarcastic laugh. 'Show them what?! That I was a fool, inadequate for the task of being a mother? It must seem incredibly cruel to you, my darling, but I gave you away because I adored you and I knew there could never a time I would be able to give you the life I wanted for you.'

'But of course you could,' Sophie said, taking her mother's hand across the table. 'Of course you could have.'

'Maybe, and maybe not. What matters now is today, here with you, a more beautiful girl I have never seen. Intelligent, caring,' Solange looked down at her hand in Sophie's, 'more mature even now than I could ever be. This has to be our moment. I don't have long.'

'How long is not long?' Sophie frowned and suddenly felt a sense of desperation.

'The cancer appears to be everywhere now. That is why I wrote to you. It took several goes before I actually sent it. I had no right to contact you after all these years and I couldn't have coped if you had rejected me. I am such a coward, Sophie.'

'No, I don't think you are, Mother. I think you have been very strong and everything you did was for the right reasons.' Sophie lifted her mother's hand and kissed it. A delicate bony hand, the skin thin and soft. Solange suddenly grasped her daughter's hand and held it against her face.

'Please forgive me.'

'Shush,' Sophie whispered.

'Gerrard wants to take me to Switzerland, he has found a clinic there. It won't make any difference but if it makes him happy for me to go, then I owe him that much. He has been a wonderful husband. We met not many years ago but these last have been my happiest. We must leave tomorrow.'

Sophie laughed inwardly at the irony. Her mother was going away again. She let the feeling pass. Solange was obviously not long for the world and at least they were together on this day.

'He can afford such treatment?' Sophie asked.

'He owns a hotel, he is comfortable, but his real wealth is in his love and kindness. Without him I would never have been able to contact you again. He gave me the courage.'

As the dramatic scenery flashed past the train carriage, Sophie thought about her mother and the short but precious time they had spent together. In the end, she had decided not to ask about her father. What was the point? He was dead.

Before Sophie went home to Versailles, Solange had asked a favour of her daughter. A final request before they parted. Would Sophie visit the place Solange had been when she called her all those years ago on her birthday, and send it her love?

How could a daughter refuse her mother's dying wish?

CHAPTER TWENTY ONE

The train eased into the station at Annecy. Sophie gathered her bags and went in search of the bus that would take her up to Talloires. She had never ventured to the French Alps before but from her mother's affectionate description of the place and the undeniably artistic scenery, Sophie reasoned maybe this was the right location to absorb and digest the last few days.

She recalled her last conversation with her mother.

'I'd stumbled across gorgeous Talloires while I was travelling. I had no plan, just worked in hotels and restaurants as I moved around. Occasionally I met a man, but nothing lasted and I'd move on again. I was so churned up that it was years before I could settle. It was only there, surrounded by such beauty, that I began to heal. I'd buried all my memories of you, they were too painful to recall.'

She stopped, struggling for breath after talking so emotionally. Sophie pressed a glass of water into her hand, but Solange waved it away.

'I let myself think about you sometimes. Not often, it still hurt too much, but just sometimes.' She smiled at Sophie, but her eyes grew distant. 'There was a birthday party at a hotel I was working in. Seeing the little girl's mother fuss over her, I just got so envious. I hated myself so much at that moment that I nearly ran out of the hotel. You see, the birthday girl was ten on the exact same day as you were ten, and I had absolutely no right to begrudge this woman her delight. It had been my decision to leave you behind and now I was paying for it all over again. Oh, I knew my parents would have treasured you as their own and given you the wonderful childhood that I had, but did I have any right to disturb that happiness and run the risk of feeling that long-buried pain once again? I knew if I didn't do it now, I never would, so I sneaked into the manager's office and called you.'

Whilst she and Sophie had walked around the bijou streets of old St Tropez, Solange had asked her daughter to visit Talloires for her because, she joked, one good Catholic should grant another their dying wish. Sophie had raised her eyebrow and questioned her mother's statement with a knowing look, to which Solange had said she agreed maybe she wasn't a good Catholic but she was a dying one.

'You didn't have to say that, Mother,' Sophie had responded.

'I did, my darling, I did.'

'Why have you never returned yourself? Especially now you have Gerrard?'

'Because until today, I never thought it possible. You see, Talloires represented you, aged ten and barely able to speak to me.' Solange caught a sense of self-admonishment from Sophie and took her hand. 'I don't blame you for that. How could I? Who was I to you then? A stranger. No, I couldn't return to that beautiful place, because you were there. In the mountains, in the moon that lit up the lake, in every snowflake that fell during winter.'

'But how is me going to Talloires a help for you now?' Sophie asked.

'Because now I cannot go back. That possibility has been taken away from me, so if you are there, then so shall I be.'

'Let's leave today, we'll go together, just a few days...' Sophie pleaded.

'My darling daughter, my time is very limited, and Gerrard has already made arrangements for us to leave for Switzerland tomorrow.'

'But... you could stop on the way, it's only an hour from Geneva!' Sophie encouraged.

'No, Sophie,' Solange put her hands to Sophie's face and smiled with an air of long-accepted resignation. 'When I say I have limited time, I mean...' she sighed, 'I have no time. The clinic will not be able to do much for me, but my husband can be very insistent, and I owe him this at the very least. I must go. I pray that one day you will meet someone as kind and caring as my Gerrard.'

Sophie collected her galloping thoughts, tears beginning to form. She looked deep into her mother's eyes and said softly, 'Then I will go to Talloires for you, for me, for us.'

Armand started up the tractor and lit a cigarette. He knew he should give them up but until his doctor ordered it so, he would try and enjoy his habit for as long as he could. The choked engine spluttered and shuddered, then found a more rhythmic rumble. He called a 'see you later' to his mother as she threw corn into the hen coup. She waved a hand to him without looking up from her task.

Clumps of dried earth and animal muck dislodged from the massive tyre treads as Armand slowly drove out of the courtyard. A grey black plume of oily diesel fumes hung in the air behind him. He looked up to the skies that were a little overcast as he made his way up to the field he planned to plough ready for planting winter crops of potatoes and maize for the livestock. August could be a month of unrelenting heat and unbearable humidity or a pleasant mixture of hot sun, gentle breezes and occasional lively thunderstorms. Armand knew which type of August this would be as sweat was already trickling down the centre of his back.

Progressing at a steady pace up a hilly road toward the field where his father waited for him to start their work for the day, Armand noticed a lone figure walking ahead of him. As he drew closer, the figure began to emerge as a tall, young woman he had not seen before, dark hair swinging at her shoulders as she strode ahead, closer still and his heart jumped.

Sophie had realised too late that she had got off the bus at the wrong stop. As it chugged down the winding hill to Talloires town and bay where she should have been, she looked across the fields in front of a small hamlet caressing the mountainside. Her map informed her it was called Perroix and, easing the irritation of her misjudgement, the map also advised it was indeed part of Talloires. Tired not only from her train and bus journeys but with the strain of her excitement and then sadness over the last few days in St Tropez, Sophie decided to take a break at a bar she could see at the edge of this charming mountain plateau community, and then take a leisurely walk around it.

As his tractor began to pass the woman, she turned her head to look at Armand, perched in the rickety seat that did little to absorb the bone-shaking vibrations of the engine. His heart was now missing beats as it leapt about like a manic grasshopper. She was the single most heavenly thing he had ever set his eyes upon.

'Bonjour, monsieur,' Sophie called up and smiled at the ruggedly handsome man gazing at her. 'C'est chaud, non?'

Armand agreed, it certainly was warm but the temperature rising in him had nothing to do with the weather. 'Mais, oui,' he responded as he bobbed his head in acknowledgement. It was about all he could manage to say without giving away that what he was feeling was causing a slight restriction in his throat. Sophie waved goodbye and carried on through the village towards the hill down to Talloires town. Armand drove on up to meet his father, lighting another cigarette, hands jittery, he dropped the match and laughed quietly at himself, lighting another.

After a very long, hot, laborious day in the field and full from eating dinner with the family, Armand settled down on his terrace with a bottle of the local red wine. He sipped the smooth but light and fruity wine, while regarding his chalet house, built mostly by himself but with help from various friends throughout Talloires, plumbers, electricians and roofers, all bringing his dream home to reality for him. Despite the homely warmth of the interior, Armand knew it could never really be a home until he added the one thing so sadly missing and his thoughts returned to the unforgettable woman he had met earlier that day.

Finally settled into a modest but tasteful hotel in the bay, Sophie walked down to the edge of the lake and out onto a partially covered wooden quay, where she knew her mother had sat many a time, just watching the gentle movements of the crystalline water. As Sophie set herself at the end of the quay and sat with long legs dangling over, in that simple moment, she could feel the enchantment of this place, just as it had bewitched her mother all those years ago. Sophie closed her eyes and saw an image of a desperate husband rushing his terminally-ill wife to a clinic for some hope but where, in truth, she would end her days. The image was so graphic, Sophie's chest constricted, and a sudden heave of emotion caused her to let out a single cry of 'Mother!' Her greatest wish then was that somewhere in her mother's heart at this very moment, she could feel this serene place again, take it with her and to have it for all time.

The following day, she decided to go back up to Perroix, find a suitable spot and make some drawings of the mountains behind it. There was so much subject matter she was spoilt for choice and ended up spending much longer, so engrossed in her workings she forgot to have lunch. A grumbling stomach insisting on urgent sustenance made Sophie finally pack up and return to the hotel. However, passing the same bar on her way, she decided to have a bite to eat there and watch the paragliders as they flew above in elegant silence.

Armand checked his watch and saw it was time to leave his rabble of friends and head for the farm to mend the tractor engine. It was playing up and his father had insisted on an even earlier start the next morning. As he walked out, he immediately caught sight of a woman sitting across at a table, looking at a menu. It was her. Early evening sunlight dancing on her straight silky hair that partially obscured her unforgettable face. Armand stood and watched her for a while and then walked over to where she sat.

Sophie's taste buds jostled for priority but the Omelette Savoyard won. She looked up, expecting to see the same charming young barman who had brought her the menu but locked eyes with the man she had seen on the tractor. He wore faded jeans and a brilliant white cotton shirt, taller than she had expected and his skin richly tanned, seeming to glow where the sunlight touched it.

'Bonjour, monsieur,' Sophie said extending her hand.

'Madame,' Armand replied supplying the briefest of hand-shakes. 'My name is Armand and we meet again.'

'Indeed we do. I am Sophie.'

Armand fought against his usual affliction of hesitation, always missing the moment where ladies were concerned. Many had tired of his dithering which stemmed from painful shyness and uncertainty of his skills with the fairer sex. It was also responsible for his empty life. From somewhere within him, his voice suddenly said, 'Are you visiting here for long?' *There, that wasn't so bad, was it?*

'I'm afraid not, only until tomorrow afternoon when I return to Paris. I would have liked to stay longer now I have found it but sadly I must go home. You are very fortunate to live in this place.'

Armand considered this. It was all he had ever known, it was his home. Fortunate? Perhaps. 'Yes, it is a lovely place. My family have lived and worked on this land for many years.' His confidence was growing. 'Where are you staying? Annecy?' He was on a roll.

'Actually, I am staying here in Talloires, L'Hotel Cygne Noir.'

Armand nodded, it was all going so well. His new-found confidence seemed to know no bounds. 'Ah, yes, a pretty little hotel. I wonder, are you free this evening?'

He couldn't help himself, despite an early start in the morning.

Sophie regarded the man standing before her, she was intrigued and yes, she was free that evening, why not? 'Yes, I am.'

Armand took a sharp silent breath and held it. The manic grasshopper was back.

They agreed he would meet her at the hotel for a drink by the lake. Her omelette arrived looking delicious, unfortunately she had completely lost her appetite.

As the train sped toward Paris, Sophie saw nothing of the undulating countryside through the window. Her mind was focused on what she should do about Didier, a lecturer who had been her lover on and off since meeting at the Sorbonne. Recently he had been indicating he wanted them to become a more permanent item, though Sophie had always said she wasn't sure, even though she did have a deep fondness for him.

Thoughts of Armand kept breaking through her musings over Didier. Nothing physical had happened at all between Sophie and Armand when they met at the hotel and drank wine in the lakeside gardens. They had just talked about everything and nothing, saying their goodbyes, never expecting to see each other again. But through the night, Sophie had lain awake, thoughts of Armand and their varied conversations, an easiness between them in such a short space of time. They had laughed much, he was a good storyteller about the life and people in Perroix, adding funny and cheeky anecdotes all the time. She had also found herself regarding his being, the way he held himself, gestured and made fun of himself. Not what Sophie had been used to. Oh, and those wonderful eyes.

The train reached the outskirts of Paris and in a strange way, she already sensed her fate had been set, a higher order having played its hand. A ruminative smile softened Sophie's pensive face. Perhaps her mother's dying wish had been rather more complex and that she had been a good Catholic after all.

CHAPTER TWENTY TWO

Just as the nutty sweetness of walnut cake passed her lips and began to satisfy her urgent craving, the phone buzzed loudly, shattering the tranquillity she had carefully created to enjoy this delicious slab of sugar and fat, bought in a nearby patisserie. The decision never to bake again made sure of that.

She grabbed the phone and snarled, 'Yes!' Crumbs flew across her desk.

'Sorry to disturb but I have Mrs Michaels down here. She would like to see you, please?' Natalie tried to sound as meek and grateful as possible.

'Offer her a coffee and give me five minutes, then send her up.' Estelle was determined to finish her cake and that unmitigated pain in the arse downstairs could wait until she had.

Mrs Michaels knocked on the door and Estelle, now suitably contented, having demolished the walnut cake, called her in and smiled radiantly at the American. Despite being heavy handed with her make-up and hairspray, Mrs Michaels was a very attractive woman with a figure to match, Estelle admitted to herself. However, a sneaky suspicion that a surgeon's knife had been at work lingered.

'Mrs Michaels, how are you today?' Estelle gushed, gesturing to a chair.

'Oh, very well, thank you for asking, and your good self?'

'Fine, thank you. To what do I owe the pleasure of your visit?' *Oh, please not another maintenance issue. It was getting more difficult to find anyone willing to go to the house.*

'Well, I was hoping to see the other young lady who helped us find the house, but I understand she's away?'

'Convalescence. Her husband died not too long ago.'

'Oh, my goodness, how terrible for her. The poor mite.' She seemed genuinely concerned. 'I wanted to give her this,' she said, taking a gift-wrapped box from her Chanel handbag and placing it on Estelle's desk. 'It's just a silly thing but she was such a sweetie and found us the perfect London home. Believe me, we had been looking for so long!'

Estelle believed.

'This is a very kind gesture, Mrs Michaels. I shall make sure Anna receives it upon her return.' The urge to ask her what 'just a silly thing' was felt strong but manners kept the question at bay, though not the little green monster rearing its head above the parapet.

'Poor Anna, I can't imagine what she's going through. One never knows how you'll cope with such an event.'

I'm sure your husband's estate would ease the blow, Estelle thought, then instantly dismissed it with a mental slap of self-admonishment. 'It's never easy for anyone.'

With Mrs Michaels departed, Estelle gently shook the box and felt its weight. It gave her no clue, so she put it in her safe, deciding she would make Anna open it in her office.

Thoughts of Anna now at the fore, she decided to chance a call to France and see how everything was going.

Unable to sleep, Sebastian sat with a strong coffee and his laptop, tapping away in communication with colleagues in Singapore and Hong Kong where the markets were open.

The first smatterings of morning light were peeking through the shutters and he decided to finish his work out on the terrace. Try as he might, it was impossible to ignore the sun rise as it crept up behind the mountains. Purples, pinks and oranges slowly giving way to hazy yellow rays spanning out like opened fingers as if the sun's hand was held just behind the peaks. A solitary bird began its sleepy morning song, soon joined by others in their secret roosts. By the time the sun peered over La Tournette, flooding the plateau of Perroix with brilliant daylight, the dawn chorus was in full melodic swing.

It made the chill Sebastian felt all the more bizarre, permeating through to his core, even under the warming sunlight. Perhaps he just needed a decent night's kip. With everything that was happening in his life at the moment, it was no surprise he couldn't sleep.

Anna appeared in the doorway. 'Morning,' she said through a yawn, stretching her arms and back.

'Morning, gorgeous,' Sebastian beamed, turning to face her and appreciating Anna's just-risen rawness. As she stretched, her night shirt rose up slightly, revealing shapely firm thighs. She caught him looking at her legs and became coy in her stance, smoothing her night shirt back down.

'I'll have a shower and make us some breakfast,' Anna said and disappeared back into the house.

Sebastian chuckled to himself at her embarrassment and returned to his dealings in the Far East but not for long, his thoughts not on business but on the lady upstairs having a shower. He couldn't help it, she was just so damned sexy and honestly didn't know the fact, which attracted her to him all the more. Sebastian would happily have continued exploring all the notions he had of them both in the shower, had his mug of coffee not suddenly shattered with a loud crack and spilled latte over his lap top.

At that moment, Anna appeared back on the terrace. 'What on earth happened?!' she exclaimed and ran to the kitchen to fetch a tea cloth. Sebastian quickly wiped the laptop with his robe and frantically checked its functions. All appeared fine, which was not how he felt. The icy chill from before had returned with a vengeance.

La Vieille Ville, with its winding stone streets, arches and canals was charming. As Anna and Sebastian meandered through the bustling ancient town looking up at the tall terraced buildings and their shuttered windows, it transported both of them to separate excursions to elegant Venice.

Selecting a small café bar in preference to the massive tourist traps along the main Canal du Thiou, they sat outside under the shadow of the Chateau d'Annecy, as it watched over the elderly town sprawl like a trusty knight.

When the wine arrived, Sebastian poured with his usual *savoir faire* and asked, 'Has coming here helped, Anna?'

She took a sip of white wine and regarded him for a beat, 'Yes... yes, it has.'

'That's good to hear,' he responded and lifted his glass in a toast to it. Little did she realise just how good it was to hear.

'Well, to some extent, I suppose.'

Not so good, then.

'It's just that I feel in understanding Max's reasons for living life how he did, it's left to me to continue, if that makes sense? You know, take life by the scruff of the neck, live every moment. What's that quote by James Dean? "Dream as if you'll live forever. Live as if you'll die today." Max must have thought I had it in me, otherwise why did he marry me?'

'I don't think there is any doubt why he married you, Anna. I can see for myself. I always have...' Sebastian stopped, he'd said too much. *Shit! Recover it.* 'When I've seen you two together, it was obvious you were a great match.' *Though not the perfect match*, he thought to himself.

'Aw, that's a lovely thing to say, Seb. Thank you. The other thing is, I don't feel my present career is right for going forward, what do you think?'

'Hey, babe, stick with me and I'll get you into the family firm!' It was in jest of course, kind of, not really, but he said it well enough for Anna not to notice. Deftly changing the subject, 'What about after lunch we hire a boat? We'll get some wine to help us along.'

'Ha ha, you drunk in charge of a boat, that's the Seb I remember!' she laughed.

'Is it?' he asked in a serious tone. 'You're right, that's exactly how people see me because that's precisely how I've lived my life.'

'What's wrong, Seb? Have I upset you? I'm sorry, I didn't mean to.'

Keeping his eyes on the bill while picking notes from his wallet, Sebastian went for the sympathy vote. 'I just feel a bit useless sometimes, that's all.'

'Well, you're not! Don't say that! You've helped me so much being here, so stop that nonsense!'

'You sound like my mother again!' he said, patting her face.

The sympathy gamble had worked. As they walked through the cobbled streets towards the lake, Anna considered whether the real Sebastian, the one only his mother knew, might be fighting for recognition finally. Perhaps Max's demise had been the trigger for him to reach out from behind the cast iron wall he lived behind most of the time. His family and social circle were not the most touchy feely of people, a vision of a black Arctic sea scattered with icebergs came to mind. *Poor sod,* she thought. Anna had met Sebastian's parents during one of their famous New Year celebrations on their vast country estate. His father had presented as friendly but somewhat dictatorial and his mother, a willowy beauty but an emotionally closed human being.

Sebastian was sent to the obligatory boarding school aged seven, mixing with other lost souls, lonely children quietly building impenetrable fortresses against the world that would remain for the rest of their lives. Expectation in excess but not love.

They reached the boat hire company and Anna let Sebastian do his thing. He did it so well. They got the best motor boat, even though it had already been reserved. Money always superseded any principles in the matter of business.

CHAPTER TWENTY THREE

The small power boat cruised noisily as Sebastian negotiated toward the Bay of Talloires. The water was smooth as they carved a path to their anchoring point. Anna sat at the point of the bow. *Eat your heart out, Kate Winslet. This is for real.*

As they approached the bay, Anna wondered if Max was with her, then decided if he had loved her as she had loved him, of course he was and that led to another train of consideration. Was it time to let Max's ghost go? Held in his own place in her heart forever but move forward without him?

They rounded the Roc de Chère and eased into the bay. Sebastian cut the engine and dropped anchor, drifting slightly until it snagged, then the boat gently came to a halt, moving on the disturbance they had caused on the water as it slopped lightly against the bow.

He rummaged in a bag and produced a bottle of champagne and a packet of paper party cups saying, 'I'm afraid health and safety determined we use these but hell, we can pretend they're crystal flutes, can't we?!' He grappled with the cellophane wrapping until all the cups tumbled about his feet. He laughed in exasperation, 'Always did like a dash of two stroke with my bubbly!'

'Absolutely! Can't beat a good petroleum aftertaste!' Anna joined in as she helped collect them.

Sebastian popped the cork and they watched it arc into the lake with a faint plop. He poured, and they toasted.

'To us?' Sebastian suggested.

'To us and our renewed friendship,' Anna concurred with that cheeky smile he recalled from times gone by.

'Yes, to that.'

They drank in silence admiring the views and the mesmerising emerald water. Anna's mind drifted back to earlier in the day before they left the house.

While they were getting ready to go into town, there was a knock on the door and Anna found Josephine and her mother standing smiling at her.

'Bonjour, Mesdames! Entrez, s'il vous plait.'

Both ladies followed Anna. Refusing the offer of a chair, Josephine said, 'No, it's just a quick visit. My mother and I, well, the family, would like to invite you to our annual village fête this weekend. We do hope you will come.'

Anna was a little taken aback but appreciated the invitation and thought it would be rude to decline.

'Ladies, that is very kind of you and yes, I would love to join you. I have a friend staying and I wonder if...'

'Of course!' Josephine said, looking at her mother and translating. A smile and nod of the head from Madame Boniface settled it. 'We shall look forward to seeing you both there. It's on Saturday and starts at midday. I'm so pleased!'

As they walked back to the farmhouse, Marie was delighted and privately relieved her invitation had been accepted. The lightness of her heart implied she had been right to take this action, perhaps helped by the forgiving hand of God. It had not been easy convincing the rest of the family, but Josephine had her suspicions about her mother's motives and it was she who finally got their approval.

Until the day came and she saw for herself, Josephine contemplated people's faces when they saw the English woman. Although Sophie had not been mentioned for some years in the village, none had forgotten the Parisian beauty who, through tragedy, had touched all their lives.

It was a risk but a calculated one. Eleanor had no intention of worrying Anna's mother but there was a chance she could help. In any case, it was Michael's idea so she could always blame him.

Since their last meeting, Michael had flown to New York for another cable television show and had told her he would try and see a dear friend and colleague while there, the one person he knew who was experienced enough to point him in the right direction, as she had encountered a similar well-documented disturbance. All this because Michael said he had to go to France, the matter had become that grave he couldn't let it run away from him. To approach it unprepared would make everything worse, much worse. So he would detour to Massachusetts where the person he sought lived in a rambling Cape Cod house, a legend in her own lifetime, Joan Golding.

Michael had attended one of Joan's seminars a few years before and she had singled him out as one with great potential. She had been generous with her praise and encouraged Michael to break into the media. Without meeting Joan Golding, he would still have been giving private readings in his flat, soon to be a small but significant house in Chelsea.

Eleanor pressed the numbers and after a few rings, the call was answered.

'Mrs Carter?'

'This is she.'

'Hello, it's Eleanor Duncan, Anna's...'

'Of course! Gosh, what a surprise!'

'May I call you Joyce?'

'Yes, of course!'

Taking a deep breath and letting it out in a long calming stream, Eleanor prepared herself to sound casual.

'I was just thinking about Anna this morning and wondered if you had heard from her?'

Odd, thought Joyce. 'Well, yes, actually I have and she seems to be doing just fine.'

'Oh, I'm so pleased! It's good that Sebastian's with her now, I worried for her being all alone out there.'

Joyce felt a sharp stab in her stomach which rose into her throat, a racing heart echoing its palpitations in her ears.

'Sebastian?' She tried not to spit down the phone.

There was a pause, then Eleanor said in soft surprise, 'Oh! I wasn't aware you didn't know, Joyce.'

'And how long has he been there? Nobody tells me anything!' *Especially my own daughter.*

Eleanor tried to extract the foot from her mouth and wished her armchair would swallow her up whole. She took a long drag on her cigarette, desperately thinking of what to say.

'Oh, please don't worry yourself, I've known Sebastian since he was a young lad. He thinks the world of Anna and she does need her friends now.'

But not THAT one, Joyce growled to herself.

'Of course, I was just surprised, that's all.' She decided to change the subject and end the call as quickly as possible. Her false cordiality only had a limited time frame. 'So how are you now, Eleanor?'

'Oh, I'm ok, Joyce.' No, she wasn't but that wasn't for Joyce to know. 'It's been lovely speaking with you again. I hope we can catch up more in the future?'

'Absolutely! Bye and thanks for asking about Anna.' Joyce hung up and looked down at Penny, sitting at her feet. 'I shall have to have words with her, Penny! I shall indeed!'

Joyce took Penny for a walk to calm herself. Maybe she was overreacting? Letting old feelings about Sebastian cast a shadow over who he might be now? Rubbish! A mother's intuition was rarely misplaced, and she knew that man had been after her daughter for a very long time. She'd seen it, stolen looks, innocuous touches, calling her 'Gorgeous' all the time, pathetic! Her daughter was bright and intelligent, why couldn't she see these things? Been blind to the fact? Max, he had been the problem from the beginning. Not only had he been a selfish bastard but a stupid one, as well. He never saw what passed for friendship but was something very different. Anna had always been very cautious with so-called friends and acquaintances. Even as a young girl, she had never had loads of friends, just a select few who had been tried and tested of her trust. Where Max was concerned, all that went out of the window and Anna was putty in his hands. That may have been so then, but this was now, and up to her mother to make sure Sebastian's covert playtime with Anna was over for good.

A bottle of champagne later, Anna and Sebastian lazed on the sun deck, in this case cheap faux white leather padding at the bow. It did its job, creating a relaxed atmosphere as they lay dozing in the sun as the boat gently oscillated on the lake.

His mind loosened, Sebastian suddenly launched into a soliloquy from Shakespeare's *Taming of the Shrew*. '*Twas told me you were rough and coy and sullen. And I find report a very liar. For thou art pleasant, gamesome, passing courteous...*' Stumbling for the rest, he managed only, '*Yet sweet as springtime flowers.*' He peeked to see if Anna was watching him, her eyes were still closed but there was a smidgen of a smile on her lips. He knew he shouldn't but he had to. He needed to know. Had to try. The timing was as perfect as he was going to achieve so he gently stroked Anna's arm. She instantly sat up and shot him a look that said, 'What are you doing?!'

'Sorry!' Sebastian held his hands up in a gesture of surrender. 'Must have been the champagne,' he said unconvincingly, then got up and went to sit at the helm.

He looked out across the bay up toward the mountains, trying to gather his thoughts. He had misjudged badly and was furious with himself. He had climbed mountains, jumped out of helicopters onto them, but right now, he needed a different courage. One that would keep him on track.

Safe within the battlements erected at an early age, there had remained a fragile core and never before had there been anyone who had been able to reach in to that tender boy, until now. Then there was a hand on his shoulder and a voice saying, 'Seb?' He looked up and met Anna's gaze.

'I'm sorry I reacted like that, it was uncalled for,' she said and squeezed his shoulder.

'I want to say I'm sorry, too, Anna, but it would be a lie.'

'A lie?'

Well, didn't he want to know? Don't hold back now.

'I love you.'

Eleanor paced as she smoked. The last thing she had wanted was exactly what she had orchestrated and she must call Anna to warn of her massive *faux pas*. Poor old Sebastian! What had he ever done to Joyce? Eleanor had never really understood why he was her *persona non grata*. He could be a bit overbearing and laddish at times but that was just him. Hadn't Max been the same? In fact, if the truth be known, Eleanor was certain Joyce hadn't much liked her son either.

She called Anna's mobile and got her message service. Eleanor would keep calling, hopefully getting through before Joyce did.

On arrival at the house, after a quiet journey from the lake, Anna busied herself in the kitchen and Sebastian went to his room to pack. It was for the best. Whilst Anna had remained cordial after his sweeping statement, it was obvious he'd blown any chance of being with her and he needed to get out of there as much as Anna most likely wanted him to but was too polite to say. As he started collecting up his things, that same eerie chill pervaded again but this time it felt as though it might as well have been the iceberg that sank the *Titanic*.

Anna picked up her messages, listening to Estelle telling her about Mrs Michaels and the 'just a silly thing' waiting for her return. Quite shocked, Anna reminded herself never to judge a book by its cover again. So unexpected. Not as unexpected as the next message, as Joyce flew at her out of the phone. *Well done, Eleanor!* she thought ruefully, just as Sebastian entered the kitchen with his bags.

'What are you doing?!' she asked incredulously.

'I think it would be best, don't you? I mean, I really messed up and I didn't come here to cause you...'

'Cause me what?! Sebastian, what are you talking about? Why are you leaving?'

'Because I feel if I don't go now, I'll lose your friendship forever,' he said, with a slight crack in his voice.

'For fuck's sake, Sebastian! I'm fine! I admit I was a bit surprised but that's all and I apologised to YOU for that! Stop being juvenile!'

'Are you sure?'

'Just take your bags upstairs and let's forget it, shall we? I'll open the other bottle of bubbly,' Anna said firmly. A slightly confused Sebastian did as he was told.

Anna hadn't been entirely honest with her friend. On

the way back to the quay to return the boat, she had reflected on why she had come to this place, her time with Sebastian here and through the years with Max. In retrospect, she knew she had probably contributed to Sebastian's feelings for her. After all, she acknowledged, there had always been a connection between them ever since Max had first introduced them. Yes, they had flirted as close friends do and in front of her husband, who sometimes encouraged his friend to embarrass his wife, all harmless fun, no?

Of course, Anna had loved Max beyond description and felt secure enough in their union to be frivolous at times. He even joked on occasion that 'at least when I go, I know there'll be a fine suitor in the wings ready to look after you.' He had always laughed at that one. Was Max laughing now? Anna certainly wasn't. To her now, it all seemed so stupid but whatever it had been, the fact remained that Anna wanted Sebastian to stay.

The madness within Armand took on a life all of its own. An energy he could feel, smell and taste. He didn't need to hear the words to know this pretender had tricked her, enticed her, was still working on taking her away. Not again. Never again. His wrath swelled and empowered him.

There was a loud, resounding reverberation in Sebastian's bedroom as he unpacked, making him stand up straight, holding his breath, looking around. For a moment, Sebastian thought maybe there had been a small earthquake, not uncommon in the Alps. Then he thought maybe it had been an electrical surge and decided to check the fuse box. He finished emptying his bags and went down to find Anna, who had opened the champagne and had started on her glass already.

'Chin chin,' she smiled, holding her glass up.

'Did you hear that?' Sebastian asked with a distracted frown.

'Hear what?'

'I'm just going into the garage to check the fuses, Anna. Make sure they're all in order.'

With that, he went down the kitchen steps into the garage beneath the house, leaving a rather bewildered Anna in his wake. As he wasn't forthcoming, Anna wondered what Sebastian had heard, he had seemed quite concerned.

In the garage, Sebastian found himself shaking uncontrollably as he checked and found the house electrics to be perfectly in order. As he turned to go back upstairs, there was a visceral feeling of something most foul standing in his way.

CHAPTER TWENTY FOUR

Even before Michael had reached the stones steps in front of her box porch, Joan Golding had swept open her double front doors, her considerable bulk almost filling the space. She stood with arms outstretched as he approached. Still the same larger than life Joan.

'Michael! My favourite student! How are you?' she said, enveloping him in a bear hug that felt like he was cuddling a big warm marshmallow, then she stood back regarding his face. Michael couldn't help but notice a huge gold Celtic cross hanging onto her voluptuous bosom.

'It's so good to see you again, Joan lovey. You look as well as ever I've seen you!' With that, Michael gave her a peck on both cheeks. 'You're very gracious to see me at such short notice.'

Her fleshy face beamed at him and Michael considered Joan could have been very attractive without the weight. However, it wasn't her physical characteristics he was interested in.

'Nonsense!' she said, guiding him into her enormous vaulted hallway. 'Come on in and let's get comfy.' Closing the doors and looking back to Michael, she added, 'No need to ask why you're here!'

Michael was startled by Joan's observation.

'Why?' he asked, with a gnawing suspicion about the reply to come.

'She's standing right behind you, honey!'

Michael felt like a bucket of iced water had dropped over him. He tried hard not to look over his shoulder. When Joan turned, he had to and of course, saw nothing.

Ushered into a huge sitting room, Michael sat on one of the three massive sofas making a square with the cavernous fireplace. Colourful rugs and architectural palms and fig plants set the room perfectly. Huge curtainless windows at the rear looked out onto sprawling grounds, edged by a thick deciduous forest. He remembered from one of her seminars that Joan loved trees, needed to live near them, explaining her belief in an ancient Greek theory about the sap in them and how these bygone people had considered it a marker of life.

As Joan wafted into her colossal kitchen, Michael noticed a rough-cut crystal on the centre of the coffee table. Diffused light filtered through the misty segments, casting different colours onto the blond polished wood. It was the most remarkable specimen he had ever seen. He watched it for some minutes as he sat back into squashy cushions, revelling in the real energy it seemed to emit, as did Joan Golding whenever she entered a room. Michael knew it was this that enabled her to be at one with the other side and it was what he now needed to learn about and fast.

Joan returned carrying a tray with herbal tea and cake. Michael recalled her addiction to cake, in fact, most things edible and delicious. She sat on the sofa and her kaftan dress billowed, giving the impression that Joan herself was not of this plane. Perhaps she wasn't, because Michael had never met another human being like her.

'Ooh! The sweet woody scent of pine,' she said while arranging cups and saucers on the table.

'I know, Joan, it follows me everywhere.'

Joan didn't look up at Michael but smiled and nodded, confirming something.

'Camomile or my own special blending?'

'I'll try your special blend, Joan lovey, thank you.'

She selected two muslin pouches from a silver bowl and dropped them into a fine bone china pot. 'Cake?' she asked.

'Not just yet, thank you.'

'Well, I gotta have some, can't concentrate on an empty stomach!'

Michael wondered if it was ever empty, then worried she might have 'heard' him.

'Come on then, honey, who is she?' Joan asked, sitting back, cake in hand, her gaze somewhere behind his head. 'Pretty little thing.'

'You can see her that clearly?' Michael said, trying not to look round like a bloody idiot.

Joan just smiled, nodded and took a large bite of cake, chewed a little, then said, 'Sure! So, Michael, tell me how she found you...'

It was half past midday and out of the blue, Anna was struck by a fit of nerves as they readied themselves for the fête. Eventually Sebastian assured her she would be fine and they started the walk up to the farmhouse. There was already a considerable hubbub coming from beneath the awning over the courtyard as they approached. Traditional country music played from a single stereo speaker hanging precariously from an old bale hook. The Boniface family held court, handling out aperitifs and simple Savoyard hors-d'oeuvres from a long wooden table.

'Doesn't get more French than this!' Sebastian said under his breath to Anna.

'I know... It's lovely, though, isn't it?'

It was. Sebastian surveyed the festive scene as they got closer, simple decent hard-working folk enjoying a get together in the most convivial way. No airs and graces, no protocol, only laughter and chatter, plus home cooked food and plenty of drink, what more did you need in life? Where he came from, too much and more, and he was sick of it.

Anna made a beeline for Josephine and was welcomed with such enthusiasm, Anna nearly burst into tears.

'Josephine, c'est mon ami, Sebastian.'

'Enchantée, Madame,' he said, taking Josephine's hand with a slight bow. Of course, his pronunciation and accent were sublime. The French woman seemed taken with his charm and was she blushing? Anna tried to hide her amusement.

Marie Boniface had watched them arrive and said a silent prayer of thanks.

Two kirs to hand, Anna and Sebastian stood to one side and observed the increasing gathering and the comradeship of the villagers. Anna noticed Madame Boniface helping arrange food on trays and their eyes met for a split second. There was a sense of something between them but when she tried to pin it down, the feeling had gone.

'Anna? Why is everyone looking at you like you've got two heads?' Sebastian asked.

'Are they?' She hadn't noticed.

'Maybe I just imagined it, gorgeous, but then of course, you are! Here's to this delightful invitation,' Sebastian toasted.

'Yes, here's to the hospitality of the people of Perroix.'

Joan munched on another wedge of her homemade carrot cake while listening to Michael's detailed account of his meetings with Eleanor. Occasionally she would close her eyes and nod and as he came to the end of his story, Michael suddenly felt as though a weight had been lifted from him, his whole being awash with relief. Joan regarded him for a moment, then smiled at him in a soft motherly kind of way.

'You poor thing, Michael. I did tell you this could happen. As I said before, you are truly blessed with the gift. Don't you worry any more, your little friend won't follow you around any longer but you've gotta help her, that's the deal!'

'Deal?' Michael enquired, trying to hide his shaky hands while drinking Joan's surprisingly delicious herbal tea.

'Yup, and we have a lot of work to do but I know you're up to it, honey.'

'Joan, I've hardly been able to sleep since, I feel totally drained,' Michael replied and looked it.

'A spirit on a mission'll do that to ya, honey... I should know!'

Because she did and that was why they were sitting in her beautiful Massachusetts home.

Stuffed with pasta, cold meats and cheeses, Anna and Sebastian sat watching the wonderful community spectacle before them, Sebastian more than anyone. His thoughts were probing deeply into a child's reflections which he'd never revealed to a single soul. How wonderful to grow up within such a place, to be an essential part of the whole. What possible troubles could you ever have, apart from the little things? How happy he might have been, a different version of the person he was now.

Anna munched on another offer of yet another locally-made cheese, the villager eager to see if it was better than the others. She pondered her relationship with Sebastian and knew whatever happened, they would always be friends. How could they not? It didn't bear thinking about. Was there room for something else? Something more physical? Or were they still wading through their previously reserved emotions, newly reopened and mistaking them for the need of an intimate relationship? *Questions, questions, enough!* she thought. *Enjoy this moment because it wouldn't come again.* This easy bon viveur. It was soothing and healing.

'Are you enjoying yourselves?' Josephine said behind Anna.

'Oh yes! It's wonderful, Josephine, thank you so much for inviting us.'

'May I speak with you?'

'Of course!'

Josephine sat next to Anna. For the few days since inviting the English woman to the fête, she had felt compelled to tell her about Armand and Sophie. She didn't understand why but he seemed constantly in her thoughts, even invading her dreams, and Josephine hadn't dreamt of her brother for many years. Why now? Perhaps he wanted this woman who looked like his wife to know his story. But that would mean he was aware of life and Josephine knew this was impossible. Nevertheless, she felt that until she told the English woman about the family history, she wouldn't rest.

She turned to Anna and glanced quickly to her mother. Satisfied that Marie was oblivious, Josephine began.

When Josephine had intervened, Sebastian had decided to fetch an unopened bottle of Highland single malt from the house. He doubted the villagers had ever had a Scotch so smooth and sweet. While back at the house, he took the chance to freshen up.

Standing in front of the bathroom mirror, he scrutinised the man looking back at him, always confident in his physical appearance, a Scandinavian paternal ancestry had taken care of that. He searched deeper. Who was this person? Since Max's death, he no longer knew. Could this man eventually succeed in having Anna as his cherished bride? Was he a worthy replacement for her beloved husband? He wanted to be, oh God, he wanted to be. He turned on the cold tap and splashed ice-cold water on his face. Refreshed, he reached for a towel and pressed it to his face. As he opened his eyes, he jumped back in horror, twisting instinctively. No one was there but there had been, a man, standing behind him. He saw him as clear as day in the mirror. Placing his hands on the sink, Sebastian shook his head.

'Jesus Christ!'

Steeling himself, he looked up again and saw only his reflection in the mirror. He felt cold again and this time, he felt it in its true form, a chill in his soul.

'Come on!' he counselled out loud, trying to bolster himself. The words of his political idol came to mind and the words 'Now is not the time to get wobbly' were said as a whisper.

Anna was astonished at the tale Josephine had told her. It was even more awful than her own recent experience.

'My mother, she hides from her feelings, but I know she still thinks you are some kind of sign. Bless her, she is old now. Since you arrived, it has made us return to those days but that is not a bad thing and it has given me reason to forgive him.'

'Forgive him?' Anna felt she hadn't been following the story completely.

'What he did, it's a terrible sin.'

'Oh, I'm sure he's at peace now, Josephine,' Anna offered, wondering where the hell Sebastian was.

And there, as if by magic, he appeared, bottle in hand. He made his way through the throng and as he reached them, Josephine stood and checked her watch.

'It is time to put my children to bed. It has been good speaking with you, Anna. Thank you. Enjoy the rest of the evening.'

'Where the hell have you been?' Anna asked.

'Fetching this to offer the natives,' Sebastian replied, trying to sound nonchalant. No need to relay what had happened in the bathroom.

'You were ages, I thought something had happened to you!'

It did actually, he wanted to say.

'Sorry, gorgeous,' he said instead and flashed his slayer smile.

CHAPTER TWENTY FIVE

Michael had called Eleanor from New York, saying he would be back in London the following day and it was imperative they meet right away. There had been a new vitality in his voice as he told her about Joan Golding and 'her invaluable help with our situation'.

It was the 'our' situation that had irked Eleanor the most, although if she were honest with herself, she was excited and yet, terrified at the same time.

Sitting quietly on the terrace drinking coffee, Anna and Sebastian separately sifted through the day. The fête continued but they felt it would be respectful to leave the locals to themselves. Everyone had been so welcoming and kind, exceeding Anna's expectations, except the bit about resembling a dead man's wife, that was spooky.

A small cloud of midges rose and fell in a spasmodic dance as the blackbird finished the last calls of his evensong and a genuine peace befell the garden. Anna looked across to a pensive Sebastian as he looked up toward Les Dents de Lanfon where, even at this late hour, two paragliders descended on fast-dissipating thermals.

'Seb? Can we talk?' Anna's voice was relaxed.

'Of course,' he replied, sitting forward and resting folded arms on the table.

'About the other day, I think we need to clear the air.'

Sebastian just lifted his shoulders in an affectionate shrug. For him, nothing had changed regarding Anna but he acknowledged this halcyon place was perhaps not quite as idyllic a place as it had first appeared to him.

'It's my feelings I need to share with you, Seb. I haven't been completely honest, I suppose, not just with myself but especially you.'

She felt a mix of feelings and emotions. Guilt, primarily but also a healthy amount of attraction to Sebastian, which, although seemingly inappropriate, caused an inward smile. Sebastian saw she was struggling to say something.

'Anna, don't say anything you're not sure of. We've had a bit to drink and look at the trouble that got me in the other day!' He so wanted to make this work and knew he had to tread carefully.

'Maybe you're right,' Anna finally said. 'I'll have a shower and an early night. Quite tiring all that effervescing! Start again tomorrow, eh?' She smiled and held out a hand, Sebastian took it and held it to his face. *Oh, Anna!* he thought.

'Sleep tight,' he said and kissed her hand.

'Seb?'

'Hm?'

'Thanks for staying. Today was lovely.'

If not now, then when?! his head screamed and something else took over his resolve. He found himself pulling Anna to him, lowering her into his lap and, finally giving up the fight, he cupped her face in his hands and drew her mouth to his.

An icy breeze swept over them but in the deepness of their moment neither felt it.

He'd never known such desperation. It echoed around his isolated world, blocking the ever-present light he kept away from. Armand called out her name in his silent prison as he watched their intimate embrace. He wanted her to hear his anguish, to feel him, to want him again.

Then in an instant, he was calm and all was still about him once more. In his unearthly consciousness, Armand, already damned and consigned to this hell, knew what he had to do.

Anna eased herself apart from their progressively sensual and searching liaison.

'Did you hear that?' she asked, looking out into the garden.

'Hear what?' Sebastian asked dreamily, not wanting the mood to be broken.

'Someone calling. I'm sure I heard it.'

Sebastian pulled her back to him and they melded again into a passionate kiss. He heard nothing because all that mattered was willingly within his arms and responding to his attentions with utter abandonment.

Michael had taken a 'red eye' flight from Boston, arriving at Heathrow in the early hours. As soon as he closed the door of his flat and dumped his bags, he called Eleanor. She answered sleepily but was immediately alert upon hearing his voice.

'Lovey, it's me. Time is of the essence. Can you come over?'

'Now? Well, I guess so, I'll be there as soon as I can.'

Now in his sitting room with a strong coffee and a selection of pastries hurriedly placed in front of her, Eleanor watched Michael as he finally settled onto the other end of the sofa.

'There's a lot to explain... Do have a pastry, lovey... Anyway, Joan's shed a whole new light on the problem, opened so much more of me. It's like she's half here and half there.'

Michael reached for a pain au chocolat.

'I don't understand, half here and...'

'Oh, sorry, I do rattle on sometimes, I know. Joan... she seems to have one foot in this world and one in theirs?'

Eleanor nodded and said, 'So what's the urgency? What is it you have to do?'

'*We*, lovey, *we*,' Michael said quickly and fixed his gaze to hers. 'I'm afraid you are as much a part of the solution as me but don't fret,' he patted her knee. 'You'll be fine! Now, do have something to eat, they were freshly baked this morning.'

'So what do *we* have to do then?' Eleanor asked, gesturing invisible quotation marks, and dutifully selecting a Danish. She had a funny feeling she already knew the answer.

'Go to the house in France.'

During their meeting, Joan and Michael had meditated together, connected with spiritual guides and come to the same conclusion. There had definitely been 'an event', a crossing over. Joan feared this was the reason Michael's visitor was becoming ever more fervent with her presence. Most likely her own husband, refusing the light and obviously frustrated in his limbo state with the equilibrium of his existence suddenly disturbed, had been strong enough to punch his way through to the living plane.

Joan knew that if they didn't act quickly, if this event was anything like the one she had lived through a few years before, lives were at stake.

Sebastian lay on his side watching Anna sleep. A strand of hair rested on her cheek and he gently stroked it out of the way. He studied every part of her restful face and luxuriated in the intense emotions now flowing through him.

He had never been so happy, he was sure. All his life he had searched for this wonderfully satiated state. Everything he had ever been through, each agony, trial and tribulation had been worthwhile. What he felt now surpassed any expectations he'd had but still something vital was missing, just one more thing that would accomplish his nirvana.

Sebastian carefully and reluctantly extracted himself from Anna's soft, warm body to go and make some breakfast for them to share in bed. It seemed the perfect start for a very new uncharted day for them both. He grabbed his bathrobe and walked as softly as he could on the oak floor boards so they didn't creak and wake her up. He carefully and silently opened the bedroom door and then all breath left him in a profound, guttural scream as he stood face to face with Armand.

Anna's eyes shot open, her body jolted by the unnerving sound of a man's cry. She sat bolt upright as the door slammed shut with a shuddering thud, then she caught sight of Sebastian, stock still and staring at the door.

Is this a dream? she thought, trying to focus tired eyes in the dim light of the bedroom. Sebastian turned and looked at Anna, his face struck with such complete horror it made her heart lurch. His eyes were wide and panicky, and she became aware of an unnatural bitterness in the air, almost tangible.

'Fuck!' Sebastian blurted out. 'As I'm standing here, he was right there!' he ranted, pointing to the door, his voice as high as Anna had ever heard it. 'Right fucking there!'

Anna was desperately trying to take in the situation and failing, the fuzziness of her sudden waking and the effects of the champagne from the night before still lingering.

'He?' she finally managed.

'The one I saw before!' he shouted, as though Anna should have known.

'For fuck's sake, Sebastian! What the hell are you talking about? You're scaring me!'

Sebastian took a deep breath and tried to appear calmer, realising she knew nothing of his previous encounter. He brushed a hand through his hair and said, 'The house is haunted, Anna.'

The moment he said it, she was catapulted back to the conversation with Josephine at the fête and a raw fear grabbed her soul. *Oh, my God!* Anna thought. *This isn't happening!*

Sebastian sat on the bed, breathing heavily.

'Seb, you're hyperventilating, slow even breaths,' Anna said soothingly, touching his arm just as he turned on her like a pit-bull.

'So would you!' he snapped, then, seeing her recoil, shook his head and said, 'Anna, I'm so sorry, you must think I've gone stark raving mad!' He moved over the bed and cuddled into her. She held him and realised she suddenly felt deathly calm, as though a protective blanket had descended over her. Perhaps it was she who was going mad, she reflected, but welcomed the feeling all the same. It was then Anna considered the horrible truth. It had been Josephine's brother in her dreams and worse, no longer confined to her subconscious, he was there with them in the house.

'Seb?' she said, while still stroking his head buried into her chest. 'If you can, tell me what he looked like?' She had to know for sure.

'Tall, like me. Dark hair, staring angry eyes and very real!' he replied and shivered in her arms.

So it was him. Anna settled back with Sebastian cradled like a child and began to tell him Armand's story.

Joan Golding lay in bed, but sleep evaded her. It was happening again but this time she was well and truly ready.

She hoped Michael had taken heed of everything she had told him. He needed to be strong and fearless and he needed to act quickly.

She entered a trance, seeking her guides, asking them to protect the couple in the house until Michael could get there.

CHAPTER TWENTY SIX

'So, you think I saw this Armand guy?'

'I do.'

Those two words touched Sebastian with the subtlety of a feather. *Another place, another time,* he thought, while she continued with her ghostly hypothesis.

'Perhaps we're just both a bit tense, what with everything, and a stressed mind can play tricks. I've heard that sometimes a troubled mind can actually start this sort of thing, though to be honest, I think he's come back, or never left. Gives me the heebie jeebies.'

N*othing like the heebie jeebies he gave me,* Sebastian told himself, recalling vicious threatening eyes. 'And don't try telling me it was a figment of my imagination! As I'm looking at you now, he was there all right. Anyway, how could I possibly be stressed after last night? Hm?' His mind drifted back to what now seemed a distant moment in time, waking up next to Anna, feeling blessed with total contentment. Mind, body and soul were, for once, in absolute harmony. 'You know, we should talk about...'

'Not on my account,' Anna interjected shyly, then giggled as she felt herself blushing. She didn't feel guilty at all, in fact strangely she felt perfectly at ease about the night before. It wasn't the same, just different and quite lovely. All she wanted to do was wallow in the sensory mood between them, taking comfort from his attentions, which last night that had left her glowing. She ducked under the duvet.

'Where are you going, you little minx?' Sebastian playfully questioned, all his senses on heightened alert again as he sought and found Anna's silky skin.

Armand was abandoned as eager mouths and bodies joined once more.

Eleanor had no choice, she had to tell her husband. Well, the bit about an impromptu trip to France, the rest was on a need to know basis and he definitely didn't need to know. Unfortunately, Renata did if she was to carry this off, without him getting suspicious. He was a shrewd old bugger, but Renata was better. It was a risk, knowing how her friend was the oracle of all gossip but a risk Eleanor was going to have to take.

The scene needed to be set without delay because she was due to meet Michael at St Pancras in less than forty-eight hours. An idea presented itself as she lit up a cigarette and blew out the first lengthy intake high up to the ceiling. Of course! She was constantly being nagged to give up 'that filthy weed' so she would be going to a special residential retreat in France to rid her of the habit. Perfect. Now time to get Renata on board, which turned out to be far easier than expected. The woman was delirious with delight at the prospect of being the linchpin in Eleanor's skulduggery. They arranged to meet later that day, leaving Eleanor the dreaded task of calling Anna and Sebastian.

While Anna showered, Sebastian caught up with some phone calls. He spoke to his contact at Citibank.

'Hey, Ollie, my man, how's it going?' He could hear the buzz of the trading floor in the background. A fleeting pang of missing the excitement of business passed through him. 'I emailed Gordy in Tokyo, did he get back to you?'

'Yup, he's interested but leave it with me, I'll get him on board. When are you back? Got a few things you and the old man might want to get involved with, exciting stuff.'

'Soon, I'll let you know when I'm inbound. Catch up then, cheers, Ollie.'

Oh, how his father detested him using such patois and that's exactly why he did. His parents lived on a different planet, the same one Sebastian was trying to keep himself as far away from as possible, with the aid of the incredibly seductive lady in the shower. But there was the irritation of their unwanted visitor and obviously, there wasn't room for both of them. Sebastian decided if he saw Armand again, it would be the spectre's last outing.

Renata listened, enraptured by Eleanor's account of her meetings with Michael. Why didn't anything like this happen to her? It was better than her Jilly Cooper bonkbusters which she devoured at every opportunity. 'How amazing' was all she kept saying, at various intervals.

When she had finished, Eleanor looked long and hard at her friend.

'Ren, this has to be just between us. It's imperative if this is going to succeed.'

'Darling, my lips are sealed!' she said, drawing fingers across her mouth.

Eleanor prayed that Renata meant what she said because it was out there now and no going back.

'I'll drive you to St Pancras and wave you off. It's so exciting, I wish I was coming with you.'

Eleanor was profoundly relieved she wasn't. Later that day, Michael called her and was dismayed that she had not yet contacted Anna.

'Well, I had to set everything up and it took all my train of thought, Michael.' It hadn't, she just couldn't find the words to tell the poor girl what was about to happen.

'Eleanor, you have to call her now. If Joan is right and she always is, whatever Anna's been through will be nothing compared to what could happen. If it hasn't already.'

A slimy chill slinked across Eleanor's heart.

'Look, give me her number, lovey, and I'll call. It might sound better coming from me, anyway.'

After a frantic deliberation on the pros and cons of doing so, Eleanor gave Michael Anna's number saying, 'Be as gentle as possible, Michael.'

Upon ending the call, Michael left a polite and professional message on Anna's message service.

'It occurs to me I have been a most neglectful host and not even made you supper since you've been here,' Anna said, as they finished a late breakfast. A lot later than Sebastian had intended that morning.

'Oh, not to worry, you've been the perfect host in other ways!' he replied, waiting for her reaction. It came, in a balled-up napkin thrown at his face.

'Anyway!' she continued, that girly shyness from earlier appearing again. 'I insist on making you supper this evening, but it means a trip into town.'

'Do I get to choose the menu?'

'I'm not one of your family chefs, matey! You'll get what you're given, sir!'

'Yes, mistress!' Sebastian smiled with a bow, imitating a doff of a hat, and they both burst into giggles as they left to go food shopping.

Alone in his house, Armand wandered. No longer able to return to his familiar quiet place, he now found himself trapped within the walls he had once lovingly built. But there was no love here now. What was once a place he held so dear, only conspired with his lost love and her deceiver to suffocate him with torment. His world was different now, no light or voices, just an abyss that was probably the gateway to 'le diable' himself. All this simply increased and strengthened his altered energy.

While salivating over the cheese selections, Anna suddenly rummaged in her bag and said, 'Blast! I forgot my purse!'

'Oh, do hush,' Sebastian smiled, 'I think I can stretch to the food shopping, gorgeous!'

'No, I want to do this properly. Could you? Pretty please?'

'Where is it?' Sebastian gave in with a good-natured sigh.

'In my other bag, a grey Michael Kors. I think it's in the bedroom or it might be...'

'I'll find it!'

Sebastian set off back to the house but passing through the lakeside town of Veyrier and while letting a very elegant lady and her equally stylish black French bulldog cross the road, he noticed an art gallery. In the window, prominently displayed, was a painting of the lake. It was a must have so he pulled over and parked.

The gallery owner was another well preserved-mature woman. *Must be something in the waters here,* he mused. She positively enthused about the local artist and although he had already decided to buy it, being the well brought up, gracious fellow he was, Sebastian allowed her to show him several other works by the same artist and discussed the various merits of them.

The painting safely wrapped and in the boot of the car, he hurried on to the house, realising he'd lost a lot of time. He had visions of Anna standing arms crossed and toe tapping at a check out on his return. He almost skidded the car on the gravel drive and quickly deposited the painting upstairs in his room. It would be a surprise for Anna over supper. Now the search for her bag which, of course, could be anywhere.

Eventually located and in the car, Sebastian realised he had left the car keys on his bed.

CHAPTER TWENTY SEVEN

Joan Golding prepared a dish of food for her seal point Siamese cat as it purred, weaving a figure of eight around her ample calves. Its long tail snaked round them like that of a macaque monkey, gripping branches high up in the rainforest canopies of southeast Asia, his occasional rasping cry an eerie reminder to Joan of his impatience.

Before the dish reached the floor, the cat greedily grabbed at the fresh chicken pieces, carefully cut into exactly-sized cubes.

'Manners, Notebook!' Joan scolded, then stood and watched him attack his meal with enough gusto to push the dish around the kitchen floor. 'Now it's Mommy's turn,' she said and perused the contents of her vast double-fronted fridge.

Somehow, Joan just wasn't hungry. Another restless night with bouts of fitful sleep, before she was woken by a strong, disturbing murmuring in her astral body, something Joan believed to be her non-physical body that occupied the same space as her material one and was directly linked to the spiritual world. For her, every living being possessed an astral self but not every living human soul could understand the concept or even want to.

During the waking periods of her disrupted night, there had been a heaviness in her vital force and a feeling of claustrophobia, all very familiar and confirming her worst fears. At least now at this stage of her life and career, she had the means to face it head on and this time had the help in the form of Michael and their mutual female ethereal friend. Joan had no doubts this woman's spirit would become pivotal to a successful outcome, but it was Michael on whom she was truly relying in her absence. He was a shining star in their field and if her prediction that morning was accurate, he had to cast his light deeper into the other world than ever before because they had just lost the first round.

Anna sat on the forecourt of Carrefour, waiting for Sebastian with rising annoyance, her trolley of goodies for that evening safely with the store supervisor who had reassured Anna that it happened all the time. However, that had been thirty minutes ago, and an hour since he had left to collect her purse. Just she thought she would abandon the shopping and get a taxi back to the house, Sebastian's car pulled into the car park.

'Where the hell have you been?!' she asked and then wished she hadn't sounded so angry, he looked so distant and perhaps a little drained. 'Are you ok?'

'Yes, I'm fine, here's your bag, sorry I was so long.'

Sebastian meant it but had no recollection of why.

On the way back, Anna chatted about the Savoyard-themed supper she was cooking that evening. Sebastian listened, granting her the occasional smile and nodding but he wasn't following the menu, feeling quite at odds with himself and concerned he'd obviously had a blackout.

After carrying the shopping in from the car, he told Anna he was going to have a lie down as he felt tired after the events of the day.

Anna checked on her messages. The first was from someone called Michael who wasn't making any sense at all and making her feel very uneasy. She saved the message, so she could listen again and try to decipher what the man was telling her. The next message was from Eleanor.

'..... he's really genuine. It's a long story but you have to be open-minded. Even if nothing has happened in the house, we must come to see you at least. Call me as soon as you hear this...'

What on earth? Anna thought.

Sebastian lay on his bed, feeling nauseous. What he hadn't told her was that he had no recollection of going back to get his keys from the bed until he was driving back with Anna's bag. It as if he had been given a shot of anaesthetic and then instantly woken, with no dream state during, just out and back. He was also unaware, as he lay on the bed pondering whether he should see his doctor when he got back to London, that his newly acquired piece of local artwork rested in a crumpled heap in a corner of the room.

In Sebastian's absence, Anna decided to call Eleanor.

'Got your message! Um...'

'Oh, I'm so pleased you've called, Anna dear!'

'I haven't a clue what's going on and who the hell is "Michael"?'

'Look, I know you're going to think I'm crazy and I wouldn't blame you if you did, but please just let me explain everything, I'm so worried about you.'

Anna sighed. 'Ok, carry on,' she said as she continued to unpack the shopping. While listening to the peculiar tale Eleanor was telling her, Anna secretly recalled the various unusual incidents she had experienced but dismissed. Earlier that day, when Sebastian insisted he had seen Armand, it had sent a very real shiver down her spine. She had to admit he hadn't looked himself when he had collected her and was certainly withdrawn on the way back, now taking a nap due to 'the events of the day'. Anna, unsurprisingly, was giving Eleanor her full attention.

'...so please let me bring Michael to the house. He's perfectly genuine. Oh, I don't know, just a feeling after seeing him about my dreams and he can help you understand far better than me.'

Anna homed in on the word 'dreams' like a heat-seeking missile locking on to target.

'Dreams, Eleanor? What dreams?'

'Dreadful things, absolute nightmares and always about the same woman, then waking with the most awful sense of dread. A friend told me about Michael and well, here we are.'

'I've also been having dreams,' Anna said quietly. 'But of a man.' She deliberated whether to tell Eleanor the next part but thought, *why the hell not?* 'From what I've heard about the family that own this house, I think it might be the man who owned it. He died...'

'Oh, God!' Eleanor couldn't help gasping.

'What?!'

'Anna, dear, it's all going to be fine, I'll see to it,' she said, trying to ease the tension, knowing full well it wouldn't be her 'seeing to it'. Then light as a feather, 'How's Sebastian?'

'Well, actually, not so good today, had a bad night's sleep and having a cat nap just n-.' She stopped mid-sentence, as something crawled over her skin in the clinging dampness surrounding her. 'Leave me alone,' she said in a low feral whisper with her eyes closed tight, 'Go away.'

'Anna?'

Anna shook off the feeling. 'Oh, it was nothing, Eleanor, more talking out loud to myself. So, when are you arriving?'

'We leave St Pancras in the early morning and with the change at Paris, I should think early evening into Annecy. When we hang up, please call Michael, won't you?'

'I will, Eleanor. Call me when you're leaving Paris with an ETA and I'll meet you.'

Anna called Michael immediately. He did sound sincere and the longer they talked, the more she became pleased he was coming to see them. He also asked both Anna and Sebastian to carry out a small task as soon as possible. It sounded rather comical but in for a penny, she thought.

Michael explained. 'Imagine pulling a hooded cloak around each of yourselves in the firm belief it is an impenetrable shroud against any harmful spirits. Please try to imagine this cloak at all times and keep the image of it at the forefront of your thoughts.'

Anna complied with his instructions and whether or not it was simply the power of suggestion, to her surprise and some relief, she felt the lingering coldness dissipate almost immediately. Now to wake Sebastian and try to explain everything, though Anna didn't feel confident he was going to take it well at all. She made some strong coffee.

Sebastian slept soundly and dreamlessly but not alone.

Inexplicably banished from her side, Armand had left Sophie and returned to the nursery while he waited patiently within the new empty darkness where he now existed, until the deceiver woke again. Time for his next illumination.

A double espresso in hand, Anna opened the door to Sebastian's bedroom. He was still face down sprawled in a star shape, deeply asleep. She felt bad, having to wake him, but knew the urgency of firstly telling him who was arriving the next day, and then, about the imaginary cloak. None of this was going to be easy and she imagined pulling her shroud tighter around herself.

As she approached the bedside, Anna saw a mess of brown paper and bubble wrap and beneath it all, a painting that was ripped to shreds. She didn't remember Sebastian bringing this with him when he arrived and why had he destroyed it? Glancing nervously around the bedroom, for the first time taking in the decor properly, she realised it could have been a child's room. She sat on the bed, Michael's illusory monk-like attire drawn closer still.

'Seb?' she said in hushed tones, while softly tapping his shoulder. 'Seb?' He finally stirred. 'I've brought you some strong coffee, we need to talk about something.'

He sat up bleary-eyed and took the mug of steaming black coffee.

'How are you feeling now, having had a nap? Better? I suppose it has been a bit of a mad day,' Anna said as he sipped his drink and rubbed his eyes. *Not as mad as it might be getting*, she thought ruefully to herself.

'Yeah, better, thanks for the coffee. How long have I been asleep?'

'You've been out for about an hour. I've been speaking with Eleanor and well... I tell you what, you wake up properly and we'll have a chat out on the terrace, it's such a lovely afternoon. Oh, yes! I meant to ask you, what happened here?' Anna said indicating the chaos in the corner.

Sebastian saw it and leapt from the bed, coffee spilling over him, the bed and the floor.

'Jesus! What the hell?' He reached down for what was left of the beautiful painting and surveyed its tattered state.

Then a thought struck him, had it been him during his black out? Was that even possible? He began to tremble but chided himself and ignored his questions, but as he gathered it all up onto the bed next to Anna, an indistinct memory popped into his head. He saw himself picking the car keys up from the bed and then a sensation of being pushed in the back. As soon as it appeared, the memory was gone.

'I bought it for you, that's why I was late getting back to Carrefour. Then I tripped on the terrace and damaged it. I was so pissed off that I'm afraid I had a strop *et voila!*'

It was the best he could think of, at that moment.

'Oh, Sebastian! Well, it's still a lovely thought, even though it's no longer in one piece, but thank you, anyway.' She reached across and kissed him, then went downstairs while not being entirely convinced by his explanation, particularly Sebastian having a 'strop' over such a silly thing and wilfully destroying a work of art.

'Michael!' Joan shrieked. 'Honey, I'm so glad you called!'

'I'm just letting you know that everything is fine for now and I shall be at the house tomorrow. I've spoken with the young lady at the house and given her your instructions regarding the psychic cloak.'

'Mm, I sense it's in place with her but not the male and it's him I'm most concerned about, Michael.'

'Ok, I'll be there soon, Joan, and I just wanted to say, I know I can do this.'

'When my famous encounter happened all those years ago, I wish I'd had you then. As I told you, you'll be real scared at times and you will doubt yourself. You'll wanna run so damn fast away from it all.'

Michael's initial burst of confidence suddenly took a nose dive, but Joan continued. 'There's something you have to hold on to the whole time and it's the most important advice I can give you.' Michael waited with bated breath. 'I wish I'd believed this fact when I went through it. They really can't hurt you if you remain firm and resolute and LET THEM KNOW IT! Until I found my inner strength, they gave me merry hell, I can tell ya! Just because they're no longer in our midst, it doesn't mean they don't have a consciousness. They're like children, Michael. Sometimes you have to show them tough love.'

'I understand,' Michael said and hoped he did, never having had much to do with children.

'There is just one last thing,' Joan said. 'I think... no, I know, you're dealing with one that's broken through.'

'Completely?'

'Well, as you know, depends on whether he's using one of them. You'll find out when you get there. You know what to do and don't forget, Michael, you always have our little friend to call upon. Another spirit from the welcome light is always a bonus.'

When he hung up, Michael sat in contemplation. This was either going to his greatest hour or, as it had been for Joan, prove to be his nemesis.

CHAPTER TWENTY EIGHT

There was a moment of silence as Anna looked at Sebastian expectantly. He hadn't said a word during her whole account of the conversations with Eleanor and Michael.

She raised an eyebrow in a mute question of 'Well?'

Sebastian's placid face broke into a huge grin, then he exploded with outright laughter.

'Oh, Anna darling!' he said, coughing from the extent of his amusement. 'A cloak?!'

Anna turned away from him and said in a tone somewhere between anger and indignation, 'You have no right to react like that, Seb! Especially after this morning.'

He stopped laughing and paused, realising he had been insensitive, and reached across to touch her hand.

'I'm sorry Anna but honestly?'

She continued averting her gaze from him to the window. Perhaps he hadn't changed after all. This was exactly the type of response she would have expected from the Sebastian of old. Anna was more disappointed than anything else, after their few days together.

'Well, I do believe there is something going on after the things I've experienced before and after you arrived. You can't deny you saw something upstairs, even you couldn't have faked that reaction, Seb.'

An unwelcome image of Armand's face and threatening, glaring eyes presented itself to Sebastian and he shook his head. 'I admit something scared me, Anna, but as you said at the time, maybe what with everything, we've both been a bit tense and I was probably still dreaming.'

Anna looked back to Sebastian and sighed. 'Maybe we should take a step back, you know, with us, until this other business has been dealt with.'

Sebastian didn't much like their union being regarded as 'business', it sounded like something his father would say, but he would reluctantly comply with her wishes. It was just another considered side step if he were to achieve his paramount aim, so he changed the subject.

'It will be great to see Eleanor again. In some respects, she was like a second mother to me.'

Slightly startled, Anna turned to face Sebastian, regarding him while reviewing her earlier character assumptions.

'Why would you say that?' It was a gentle enquiry.

Sebastian got up from the sofa and walked over to the window, looking up at La Tournette.

It was time to go for broke, open up, why keep the drawbridge firmly down if he wanted to spend the rest of his life with this woman? Yes, he ran the risk of losing heavily and paying the price emotionally but no pain, no gain was his mantra while speculating on a volatile market and definitely no wife.

So he spoke of lonely weekends at school, when most of the other boarders went home on exeat, his father almost always in the Far East and his mother sunning herself at their villa in the south of France. Occasionally Sebastian would spend time there and recalled the gaggle of bohemian friends who would visit, sometimes his mother going off with them for days at a time, leaving him with the house staff to entertain him. When his father did make an appearance, it was usually for the Cannes film festival and it was during a reception one year that Sebastian lost his virginity to the daughter of a French film producer. He told of them sneaking out from the raucous party to a small beach where he was also introduced to her considerable oral talents.

When he wasn't at school, at summer camp or with his parents, he would spend a lot of time with Max's family and grew close to Eleanor, who showed him the affection and caring so lacking from other quarters.

'So you see why I said what I did about Eleanor. I guess most wealthy families like mine have some mad old aunt in the attic to turn to, but I had Eleanor!' Sebastian chuckled at this, but it was to screen the fact he was entering dangerous territory and time to put that box away again for another time. He had said more than he had expected to and hoped it hadn't been too much too soon.

'Oh, Seb, why, after all these years, didn't I know any of this? Why haven't you told me until now?'

Why would I have? he thought.

Anna could sense a reserved air with him and said lightly, 'Well, I'm going to do some prep for supper. What about you?'

'I might go for a walk, do you mind? Clear my head.'

Anna smiled and gave a little wink of agreement. Sebastian left her busy in the kitchen as he set off for a stroll around the village.

As she sat on a bench facing east looking out toward The Seven Sisters, Joyce watched Penny running nose to ground in her usual ever-decreasing circles. The sky was spotted with cotton puff clouds that dimmed the sun's heat as they floated across its mass. The sea was murky from the gusty winds the previous night and Joyce noticed a new chalk fall on a small beach cove near Birling Gap. It brought memories of great family debates about global warming, instigated by her daughter, and one particularly heated discussion which ended with Anna shouting at her father, 'You just don't want to face the truth, do you?!' Joyce smiled, her daughter had always been so passionate about things she believed in and at least that hadn't changed, whereas so much had.

High-pitched yelps brought her focus back to the cliff top and Penny, scampering around a couple of small poodles which in turn were chasing her. Joyce called to the dog and she obediently responded and sat at Joyce's feet, tongue dangling from a huge panting smile.

Anna had filled Joyce's head since she had left that irate message, which she now bitterly regretted. She was well known in her family for such outbursts, especially where Anna was concerned, followed by a terse, silent standoff, before one of them would pick up the phone and all would be well again.

Max eased himself into Joyce's mental ramblings. Despite his stupid need for dangerous sports and dubious friends, he had made Anna very happy and so her daughter now suffered the consequences of his death more deeply than she could bear at times. Then Sebastian blagged his way to the forefront of her thoughts and Joyce sighed.

'What am I to do, Pen? I can't sit back and watch Anna make the worst mistake of her life, can I? What do you think?' Penny looked at Joyce, the dog tilting her head from side to side as she listened to Joyce's words. 'I know exactly what you think,' Joyce said, getting the lead from her pocket. 'Din-dins!'

Penny's ears pricked up and she started prancing about like a kid goat until Joyce managed to finally get the lead attached and made for home, with the intention of calling Anna to make amends for the message.

The train pulled gracefully to a stop in Gare du Nord, Paris. Eleanor and Michael immediately checked on their connecting train to Annecy, before calling Anna to advise of their timings.

During the journey to Paris, Eleanor had asked Michael why he was so eager to help with the situation. His response had been pragmatic. In one way, he had little choice in the matter if he were to start functioning normally again for other clients, his channels skewed and held to ransom, there was little room for anything else. He also explained that his psychic ability was a gift and should be given graciously if and when called upon, especially in urgent circumstances such as this. There was another reason and that was Joan Golding herself, a more powerful intermediary between the spiritual and mortal planes you would not find and if she was concerned, then he had to act where Joan could not.

Eleanor thanked him for his candour.

'Don't thank me yet, lovey!' he said, 'Much to do, much to do.'

The phone rang again.

'Yes!' a frustrated Anna said. At this rate she wouldn't get the supper on.

'It's Mum.'

'Hello, Mum! Sorry, I was cooking...'

'Oh, then I'll let you go and call...'

'No, no, Mum, hang on a minute,' Anna said and grabbed a tea cloth to wipe her hands of flour. 'I can always talk to you!'

Joyce apologised for her earlier rantings and a loving truce was easily declared. After ending the call so Anna could get on with supper, Joyce felt a penetrating chill sweep over her. She cast it aside as being connected with her continuing misgivings about Sebastian, now dutifully held in check but in readiness for airing at an appropriate time.

CHAPTER TWENTY NINE

While the others chatted out on the terrace in the softening heat of the day, about something and nothing, delaying the truth of why they were there together, Michael wandered quietly through the house alone. In a deliberate manner, he went from room to room, absorbing the energies present until he found the one that didn't belong there.

The atmosphere was oppressive throughout, but it wasn't long before Michael stood in what he believed was the focal point for the hopeless soul he sought. The intensity of the room's aura was palpable, but it was the strength of the wretchedness pervading the atmosphere that nearly took his breath away.

On the terrace, Eleanor and Anna conversed nonstop. At the station when Anna saw her mother in law's smiling face through the stream of passengers coming toward her, she realised in a sudden burst of emotion how much she missed her own. Now she sat devouring Eleanor's company. Sebastian gave an occasional nod of the head or monosyllabic response but mostly watched their animated dialogue in silence. In truth, he was far from this place, wrestling privately with huge internal conflict.

He needed to establish a clear train of thought and dispel an uncharacteristic and slightly disturbing sense of not being in control, of being sucked into a realm that until now he had positively rejected. There was no doubt in his mind he saw a man when he opened the bedroom door - but a ghost? The more he had thought about the incident, the more he had settled on the conclusion it was a dream, one of those night terrors he had heard about from friends but, as far as he could recall, had never experienced himself, until then. The descriptions they relayed of panic-stricken partners trying to wake them, led Sebastian to believe it was entirely possible for him to have scared himself and consequently, Anna, in the way he had but it was the effect this was having on their fledgling relationship that troubled him most.

Anna's request that they 'take a step back' had played over and over in his mind, his analytical brain trying to reach a satisfactory explanation and failing miserably. This was no business deal and in opening up to Anna about his life, he had caused a fissure within his emotional fortress that allowed a slow release of doubts and fears into a normally tight-ship mind. Here was the only woman he had truly ever wanted and assumed would never be his but through the tragic loss of his friend, she was now within reach. On the threshold of achieving a dream, it was apparent he was beginning to lose the plot.

During his walk around Perroix, he had felt as though he were being followed, such a strong inkling that he kept looking around. By the time he had returned to the house, it was replaced with a deep foreboding. Although Anna had produced an accomplished Savoyard supper of a local fondue recipe, served with cold meats and potatoes instead of day-old crusty bread, and they had both laughed fondly about past times with Max, Sebastian couldn't shake an odd sense of doom. For him? For them? It would not relent and had remained with him ever since. He began to think maybe it was a demonstration of the festering guilt he kept contained in the dungeons of his conscience regarding

Max, whether about his involvement in his death or the path he set out on to capture Anna. A malevolent reminder that, at the outset of his pursuit of her, he might pay dearly for it. But Sebastian knew she was worth risking his soul for and he would do whatever it took to honour the pledge he had made to himself to finally bring genuine happiness into his life.

Michael re-joined them on the terrace and approached Sebastian.

'May we have a quick chat?'

Sebastian regarded this odd little man with considerable suspicion but complied and said, 'Of course, let's go inside and leave the ladies to themselves, shall we?'

Once seated at the dining table, Sebastian smiled at Michael, waiting to see what he wanted to talk about, all the while wondering why the hell he was putting up with this charlatan interfering in his life.

'I understand from Anna that there was an incident with a painting you purchased?'

'Well, yes, but I don't think it's anything...'

'I'll be the judge of that,' Michael cut in with an air of authority he was unfamiliar with. 'Would you show me where this happened?'

'Very well,' Sebastian said.

As they climbed the stairs, Michael knew already.

'Good heavens!' Eleanor exclaimed. 'Look at the time! We need to get a move on, I haven't even unpacked yet!'

'It's so lovely having you here,' Anna said and hugged Eleanor, then decided in the men's absence, to tell Eleanor about herself and Sebastian. It would most likely present itself at some point and she would prefer Eleanor to know now and have time to deal with it, hopefully well.

'Eleanor, there's something I need to say.'

'Oh? What would that be?'

'This might be upsetting but it was never meant to be,' Anna started to flounder immediately.

'What is it?' Eleanor smiled kindly. 'I'm a big girl, let it out!'

'Me and Seb, it wasn't planned and...' Anna stopped and searched Eleanor's face for a reaction. She appeared to take a long, deep breath while her eyes remained fixed on Anna's. In the pause, the sound of the blackbird singing his haunting evening monologue filled the garden, yet sadly at that moment seemed inappropriate.

'I see,' Eleanor finally spoke.

'I'm so sorry,' Anna started to cry.

'Oh, Anna,' Eleanor sighed and reached out for Anna's hands. 'I can't say I'm not a little surprised but my dear, you are a lovely young woman and life moves on, I know that. I suppose, in a way, I shouldn't be surprised at all.'

Anna saw tears in Eleanor's eyes as she looked out into the garden to the fir tree that she had been drawn to the moment she arrived and the bird song emanating from where it stood.

'Just as long as you know what you are doing and don't get hurt. God knows we've all been through it and you most of all. It's natural to crave comfort but just be careful.'

Anna nodded and, after wiping their tears and affirming their friendship, they headed into the house. As they reached the door, Eleanor turned and looked across the garden again.

'Isn't that a beautiful tree!'

Anna carried on into the house and simply said, 'Yes it's lovely', while a shiver touched her spine as she recalled the dreams.

Michael stood in the centre of the bedroom, looking at the painting Sebastian had found difficult to touch again and therefore throw away.

'So, what happened here?' Michael asked.

Sebastian shrugged and replied in a slightly mocking tone, 'I dropped it, ok?'

'Dropping it wouldn't have caused such damage.' Michael shot a disdainful glance at the tall fair-haired man standing in the doorway. It was becoming ever more apparent to him why this sham of an individual had unwittingly become an instrument in a desperate soul's deadly game. 'I think perhaps I might be better informed.'

'Sorry, it's just I find all this a bit... Well, I don't know.'

'I'm not at all surprised by that.' Michael's tone was returning to somewhere close to friendly. 'What we are dealing with here is very real and even more angry. I know you didn't drop this, the energy that did this wasn't doing it to spite you, it was doing it to spite itself. This subject matter provoked something within its consciousness and this is the result.'

Sebastian just looked at Michael. He had the same passing memory as before but refused to get dragged into it, but Michael had other ideas.

'Anna told me you had a blackout? Or something like that and afterwards you found the painting in this mess?'

Cheers Anna, Sebastian mused. *Not helpful.* 'It seems so,' he said with an edge to his voice.

'Look,' Michael said, 'I know you don't go in for all this, but I assure you there is a presence in this house that requires guidance to the spiritual realm. For some reason, it is stuck here and getting extremely frustrated. We'll start work tomorrow but I suggest no one enters this room again until then, especially you.'

Sebastian tried to look sincere in his acknowledgement but inside, he was desperately trying to hold back laughter. 'I'm sure that's fine,' he said, 'I'll go and tell the ladies.'

He was delighted to be released from this pathetic man and blatant money-making farce.

Michael gently placed the painting remains on the bed, adjusting them as well as he could to reveal a misty representation of the lake. He closed his eyes and for a moment, he was silent, then in a kind and caring tone said, 'I feel your pain, sense of injustice and most of all, your loneliness. I am here to help you, but you must help me too. You can leave these mortals be, you have no need of them now. There is a wonderful light waiting for you. Friends and family are in that light. Let all your hatred and self-loathing vacate your soul and prepare for the final journey.'

CHAPTER THIRTY

'Tell me everything that has happened since you arrived here,' said Michael, as he appreciatively sniffed the supper Anna had just placed before him.

Glancing at Sebastian, Anna said, 'Well, it started with the nightmares...'

Michael listened attentively.

'...and that was the most bizarre of all,' she concluded, recounting what happened the morning after they had, as she put it, spent the night together. Michael tilted his head and nodded slightly with a little smile, while Sebastian held his breath and tried to sneak a glance at Eleanor. She was looking straight back. He stopped chewing on a mouthful of *pommes dauphinoise,* knife and fork suspended above his plate and became a still life of a guilty child.

Eleanor frowned, pursing her lips, but then softened them into a smile to say *I knew*. It was an awkward few seconds and showed Anna, who had seen the exchange, that Sebastian still had a healthy respect for Eleanor.

Anna took a good swig of wine and a long intake of breath as if to say, *finally it's out there*. Then Michael brought them up to speed with his own findings and those of the eminent Joan Golding. By some freakish coincidence, Sebastian had watched Joan on television in his room at The Waldorf in New York, whilst he was preparing for a dinner meeting with the owner of a leading venture capital company, a Wall Street baron he was trying to negotiate a merger with on one of their newly acquired businesses. Sebastian had sat on the bed putting his socks on, and was incredulous people actually believed such shit. However, when Michael mentioned her name, he kept the memory to himself but decided enough was enough. He simply wanted to extract Anna from this ridiculous set up.

Mostly he was shocked that Eleanor, a straightforward no nonsense lady who always said it how it was, now seemed thoroughly entranced by this confidence trickster, delving into things she should be leaving well alone. He forgivingly put it down to her grief over Max but the thought of his friend brought back that feeling of doom which he deftly consigned to the back of his mind again.

When Eleanor and Michael left for a hotel in Talloires, Sebastian was sent to sleeping on the sofa which grated. He had thought, as they were alone in the house, Anna might relent. He would have to up his game, he only had a few days left before business and his father insisted on his presence.

The following morning, Michael and Eleanor arrived early and, having been given a key by Anna, found Sebastian still slumbering in the sitting room. Eleanor gestured she would make some tea and Michael sat at the dining table, observing the peaceful form on the sofa and pondering his labyrinthine and unfulfilled character.

Anna had heard them arrive and joined them. The general chat finally woke Sebastian who stretched his long frame before sitting up with his back to the rest of the room. He wouldn't spend another night like that with the indignity of being woken by the slimy individual called Michael whose eyes he knew bore into his back.

All seated at the kitchen table, with croissants and coffee, Michael explained what they were going to do and that they should be prepared for anything. Sebastian inwardly sighed, trying to keep his cool. At some point, he must get Anna alone and speak with her. They both had better things to do than listen to this unmitigated twaddle, especially as he had a weird feeling that Anna was slipping from his grasp.

Michael produced a holdall and gave them each a large white candle, one to be placed in each room and lit. He explained this would represent the light he wanted to flood the house with. In silence, they took their candles to different rooms, Michael to Sebastian's, and then congregated downstairs. Michael closed the curtains, lit another candle on the dining room table and some joss sticks, the aroma of which Eleanor remembered.

'We must cleanse our minds of negative thoughts, open ourselves to all possibilities and welcome them,' said Michael, glancing at Sebastian. 'This higher state of mind will empower us in the task ahead. Let's all join hands in a symbolic circle of strength, close our eyes and quietly meditate.'

Sebastian had to work hard to contain himself but an inappropriate giggle was pushing forward all the time. *You're doing this for Anna,* he instructed his inner irreverent child, *for the future Mrs Petersen.*

Eleanor's heart pounded as she worked hard to clear her mind but the woman by the lake in her dreams was ever-present. For several minutes, they remained in tranquil reflection while the candles flickered throughout the house. The precarious calm was shattered by a chilling crash from upstairs. No one moved but wide eyes exchanged looks, they had all heard it. Even Sebastian felt uneasy because the noise was directly above them, his bedroom, and this time, he knew it wasn't an earthquake or electrical surge.

Michael spoke first while the others looked like startled rabbits.

'It's started. Now you must all remain calm and keep your thoughts clear. Do exactly what I say and when I say it, even if it means doing something you feel uncomfortable with. Pay attention to me at all times, is that understood?'

They all nodded and, more terrified now than she ever been in her whole life, Anna just felt numb. Sebastian was at a loss what to feel, trying to distance himself as his inner turmoil was reaching fever pitch. He so wanted to support Anna, show willing. Of course some weird shit had gone on but this whole spectacle was totally at odds with his psyche, he had to draw a line to preserve his own sanity.

Michael left the table where the fluid flame of the candle at the centre of it scattered a fluttering yellow glow upon their faces. An aroma of sandalwood from the joss sticks permeated their surroundings. The atmosphere was so dense you could have reached out and grabbed it.

CHAPTER THIRTY ONE

Two weeks after returning to Versailles, the call she dreaded but knew was imminent arrived during a particularly crisp sunny morning.

Gerrard, as promised, called from Switzerland to tell Sophie her mother had died in a morphine-induced sleep, slipping peacefully away from pain with dignity and grace.

'She looked remarkably beautiful in her passing.'

'Thank you for being with her and for bringing light to the last years of her life.'

'You and the family are welcome to stay at my home in St Tropez for the funeral.'

Sophie thanked him and prepared herself for the task of telling her grandparents.

Isabelle and Maurice were initially distressed that their daughter would be interred so far away from them but as Sophie said, it was where she had finally found happiness and they were comforted by that.

The date was set and prior to leaving with her grandparents, Sophie went to Paris to meet Didier. It was time to let him go as well. They met at their regular place on the Champs Elysees and true to form, Didier arrived with an armful of flowers. The centrepiece was a huge arum lily. 'For your dear mother,' he had said, making her task even more difficult.

It had occurred to Sophie that her mother's passing was not an end but a beginning. With lingering thoughts of Armand and the vital life he led, working the land in that unforgettable setting, she had decided it was time to start living her own life in accordance with her inner voice. Since her mission to Talloires on behalf of her mother, that voice had been persistent and was getting louder. Of course, it was a risk returning to Talloires and possibly her handsome farmer. They had only met twice but there was more certainty about that future than she had felt for any other. Therefore, Sophie would take a detour on the way back from the funeral.

With the cooler evenings of autumn upon them, Armand began stockpiling the family's fire wood for the winter. Part of the land they owned included a considerable amount of forest and he had been logging all day in the courtyard. It was arduous work and, quite exhausted, he returned home after dinner at the farmhouse.

Lighting a fire to cheer him, he watched the infant flames as they caught hold and set a relaxing glow throughout the room. He listened to the reassuring cracking and spitting of the wood while absorbing the comforting ambience it generated. As Armand gazed into the constantly changing life of the flames, his utter loneliness was never far away and had recently been made worse by memories of the lovely Sophie. There had been something about her, releasing unknown emotions in him, and yet he sat there, alone once again but not for long. He smiled to himself, it was only for one more night.

An unusually frosty morning greeted Armand as he started up the tractor, ready to deliver logs to various family members and villagers who paid a nominal tariff for them. After that, he would take the short drive up to Thones, a small picturesque town settled higher up in the mountains. There he would collect his new friend, a golden Labrador puppy he had already decided to call Leffe, after the golden beer of the name and a favourite of his.

In St Tropez, Sophie said goodbye to Isabelle and Maurice as they set off on their journey back to Versailles. It was a few hours until her train to Annecy.

The funeral had been quite an elaborate affair, nothing too much for Gerrard's Solange. They all agreed she had been a very complex human being and in a way was still there with them all, living through Sophie. Isabelle and Maurice had been grateful for the sensitivity in the planning and detail of the ceremony and private gathering afterward. They told Gerrard they were sorry not have met him before their daughter passed but said he was always welcome whenever he visited Paris.

Returning from Thones with an over-excited Leffe in the Land Rover, Armand decided he would show her off to his friends in Le Cantonnier, drinking a toast to Leffe's arrival with her namesake seemed fitting. He parked up and carried the wriggling bundle towards the bar, then suddenly stopped. Leffe seemed to sense the change in his demeanour and also became still. Sitting at a table sipping a coffee was Sophie.

Six months later, they stood at the altar of the ancient church of Talloires. Already legally married at l'Hotel de Ville in accordance with French civil law the previous day, they slowly progressed through the lengthy Roman Catholic wedding ceremony. In their hearts, they had been a union from the first day they met.

As church bells confirmed their marriage, Marie Boniface quietly watched as Armand left the church with his bride, amid a shower of rice and rose petals and felt a strange emptiness. This girl wasn't just unsuitable as a wife for her son, she was wrong on all counts, a city girl and a country man? How could it be so? Marie knew she must believe God had brought them together for His own reasons and who was she to question the workings of His greater plan? Even so, she wasn't happy about it.

The celebrations were unlike anything Perroix had seen in years, Jacques and Maurice sparing no expense. Secretly Jacques liked this lively woman who had finally brought a much-needed radiance to his eldest son's soul. He was well aware his wife wanted Armand to marry a local girl who understood the ways of the mountains and their people, but Jacques suspected that no woman would ever have made the grade where her first born was concerned. Most importantly, Sophie seemed devoted to his son and as a father, he could not have asked more of her.

Isabelle and Maurice had at first been shocked and alarmed that their precious grandchild was about to embark on a completely different life from the one they had been guiding her towards. History seemed to be repeating itself. It took a visit to meet Armand and place where she would live as his wife that helped to calm their fears, but both still held a doubt. He was a decent hard-working man, not wealthy but comfortable, his riches coming from more fundamental things in life and in a way, it reminded Isabelle of her own father, but there remained an uneasiness about it all.

Now sitting there watching the newlyweds taking their first dance, there was just a small regret in Isabelle's heart, that Solange was not there to see her beautiful little girl as a stunning bride and completely happy. Then she smiled, being quite certain that Solange had been there all along.

Leffe shadowed Armand's tractor on his return home from a day ploughing fields as she always did, even to the edge of the village where she would know to stay behind and wait for him, sometimes sitting for hours at the entrance to the farm. watching the road until he returned. Sophie adored the dog and had already produced many drawings and water colours of the various stages of her life. It was while she was finishing another that Armand finally collapsed into his armchair and Sophie brought him his shot of Ricard. He smiled wearily as his wife kneeled in front of him.

'Hard day?' she asked, knowing the answer.

'As always, my darling, as always,' he responded, stroking Leffe who had sat beside him.

'I have something to tell you, Armand.'

'Oh? So, tell me then!' He smiled at his wife and held her look while sipping the Ricard.

'Well, I saw the doctor today and...'

Armand sat forward, set his drink down and cupped Sophie's face.

'And he said?'

'I know what your Christmas present will be!'

Armand was overwhelmed, kneeling down from the chair to take Sophie into his arms.

'My clever wife!' he exclaimed, tears falling freely. 'My beautiful, clever wife!'

Didier had wrestled with the decision for weeks but in the end, he knew there was no choice but to make a new life for himself away from Paris and the spectre of Sophie everywhere he went. An offer to work as head of department at a university in Montreal, Canada had been confirmed that morning and Didier had accepted. He had been to the city several times and it had left a lasting impression, although he would never have predicted starting over there in his middle age.

There remained one decision to make and it was the most tortuous. Did he contact Sophie and let her know and tell her he had a special goodbye gift for her, should she wish to accept it A painting he had worked on for months. It was of a particular spot in Paris that was dear to both of them.

Surveying her design so far in the nursery pleased Sophie. She had so many ideas and there was only so much wall space to work with. After trying to help, Armand had left it to her. He was no artist and now she was pregnant, her stubborn streak was getting worse by the day. Nevertheless, he knew she would create the perfect place to bring their new child home to.

She was engrossed in completing a group of farm animals when the phone rang.

'Sophie?'

There was a moment's silence while she collected her thoughts.

'Didier, my goodness! What a surprise...I don't understand. How...?'

'Please don't be angry but I asked your grandmother for your number. It's important we speak.'

Sophie would have to make sure Armand did not find out about this.

'I will deal with my grandmother in time, Didier, but why are you calling? We parted good friends and I have a new life now. Please respect that.'

'Can we meet one last time?' He was almost begging which was not the Didier she recalled.

'I don't think that is possible.' Sophie knew it wasn't.

'I am leaving for Canada soon and I will not be returning.'

The words affected Sophie more than she had ever expected them to after all this time. They had known each other for years and although living different lives, there was always going to be a connection through their art.

Even now when viewing her work or that of others, she would surmise what her old tutor's opinion and suggestions for improvement would be. There was also a distant suspicion that his move to Canada was born from their parting.

'I will see what I can do, Didier, but I cannot promise. I will call you.'

Perhaps if she explained in simple terms to Armand, he would understand and have no fear about meeting one last time just to say goodbye and tell him of their happy news.

'No!' Armand boomed across the kitchen, his face contorted with rage. Leffe got up from under the table and ran down into the garage. Sophie tried to placate her furious husband.

'Please Armand, my darling, it's just a final request of a friend, that is all. I am your wife and will always be. I carry our child. You are my world, and nothing and no one will ever change that.'

'I said no!' Louder this time.

Something in Sophie felt this attitude was unnecessary and quite unfair, if not a little immature. She knew what a jealous and possessive man Armand was where she was concerned. He simmered at times but he had never let it boil over like this. Then suddenly she decided yes, she would go to Paris and call in to see her grandparents on the way.

'Darling, I never thought I would go against you but in this instance, I must. You are being ridiculous.' With that, she left the kitchen and went back to the nursery.

Armand looked at his headstrong wife as she walked defiantly away. He had always wondered when her hard-hearted city life would rear up and bite him and now it had. He had tried so hard to be a liberal-thinking husband, balancing that by showing a degree of authority he believed was necessary from a husband. When it mattered, it had failed.

The next day, he watched from a high field as Sophie turned her car onto the main route out of Talloires and headed north.

'I should have been a man and seen her off, Leffe. Instead I sit up here with my pig-headed ideas and didn't even say goodbye. How stupid am I, my little friend? How stupid am I? God keep her safe.'

He made his way back to the house which felt colder and lonelier than it ever had before Sophie had arrived. Leffe searched all the rooms for her and settled in her basket with a resounding huff while Armand started to make some breakfast he had no stomach for.

An hour later, Sophie's crushed body lay in the crumpled wreckage of her Peugeot underneath the twisted bulk of a container lorry.

When the graveside service was over, Armand waited for everyone to leave and stood alone, staring into the pitiful hole before him. There, framed by the cold dark earth, was an ornate coffin containing the light of his life and their unborn child.

For the first time since learning of her death, he began to sob uncontrollably, falling to his knees with his head in his hands. His cries became grotesque screams that brought the priest quickly to his side, bending down to comfort the man but pushed away. Father Luc gently told him he would not be far away and left the distraught figure alone.

It was as though Armand's soul had been ripped from within and lay in the same grave. For as long as he lived, he would never forgive himself for letting Sophie drive away that day without telling her he loved her and was sorry.

The accident was his fault. She had not been thinking clearly because of him, not concentrating on the road.

He also knew his prayer to the Lord as she had left had gone unheeded.

CHAPTER THIRTY TWO

Michael opened the door to the room which had obviously been a child's room. with beautiful images of animals. He was immediately touched by iciness. It settled on his skin like the clinging damp sea mists that roll in. The bed was upturned with a jumble of bedclothes underneath. *So much fury*, thought Michael. *So much despair.*

He stood very still and meditated into a trance state ready for contact. Joan's words about wanting to run away brushed over his clarifying mind. As usual, her prediction was accurate but Michael wasn't backing away now and he sent that message loud and clear to Armand.

As he opened his eyes, having found the higher consciousness he sought, they focused on one corner. There was a disturbance in the natural vibration of the air, nothing obvious to the untrained eye, no physical manifestation but a feeling that drew Michael's attention. He walked slowly into the room, speaking as though to soothe a troubled child.

'Let me help free you from here. You don't belong in this house any more. See the wonderful light.' Michael reached his hand out towards the candle that was flickering unevenly, the flame sometimes reaching a seemingly impossible height. 'Welcome the light.' He paused again. The disturbance increased and he sensed a distinct change in the aura, which quickly became more oppressive.

Michael could feel waves of emotions beating against his own vital force and a tear collected at the corner of his eye, as he recalled Joan saying it might happen if he truly reached through to this desolate soul. She told him not to hide his emotions but open them up and let it see that Michael understood the agony it had felt for so long. Armand couldn't, so the medium must cry for him. In doing this, he might draw the presence out from what it considered a safe hiding place. Michael spoke again.

'There is nothing to keep you here. Your family's in the light, waiting to guide you. Let go of the darkness and step into the light.'

His voice was taking on a commanding quality, following Joan's instructions. Then Michael heard him. A name, over and over, filled his head and jangled his senses, flowing through him like an electrical conductor.

Michael responded instantly. 'Sophie is not here.'

There was a clatter as the candle fell onto its side, rolled across the bureau and dropped to the floor. Michael picked it up and relit it, placing it back on the bureau with shaking hands, hot wax dribbling down onto his hands. He walked to the doorway and called to the others, who all looked at each other, then at Anna, as Michael called her upstairs. Sebastian touched her hand as she got up.

'Do you want me to come with you?'

'No. I should go alone.'

Anna didn't know why but she was adamant and closed the sitting room door behind her. Eleanor looked at the bewildered and increasingly fractious man across the table. He was having difficulty containing himself but he had to.

'It'll be over soon, Sebastian, and we can all go about our business as normal again. I promise you.'

He kept his gaze on the table and said, 'Maybe.'

As Anna reached the landing Michael instructed her not to enter the bedroom. She stood looking into it, trying to disguise her horror at the sight of bed lying upside down, finding it hard to control her breathing.

'Who is Sophie?' Michael asked, still facing into the room.

'His wife,' Anna replied shakily through a rapidly drying throat.

'She died in that accident?'

'Yes, as far as I know.'

'And Armand?'

Anna didn't know if her nerves could take much more but she stood fast.

'I was told that he killed himself.' She wanted to weep but couldn't, her terror was overriding every emotion within. Michael tilted his head as if considering something and picked up the tattered painting.

'This is where he died, Anna. In the lake. This picture reminded him of his terrible deed, so he destroyed it.'

'Why? How?'

'He loathes himself. It's what keeps him here but there is also something else.' Anna didn't want to hear 'the something else'. She had seen and heard enough already. 'From what you have told me about your dreams and the other stuff, I am quite certain he believes you are Sophie.'

So did Joan.

Anna swayed slightly and held on tight to the bannister. All breath seemed to have left her now as Michael finally turned to see the alarm in her eyes.

'He won't hurt you, Anna, he never would have. Sebastian is another matter.'

'Sebastian?!' Anna whispered, while desperately wanting to run back downstairs and into his arms.

'The entity perceives him as a threat and now you have become lovers...' Michael trailed off and turned back into the room. He could feel Armand reaching out toward her, grasping for Sophie. The hopelessness was palpable and

Michael swallowed a choke of emotion. The room filled with a bitter-sweet feeling of wanting so badly and being so close but unable to have. It was time to call upon the persistent spirit he now knew to be Sophie. Michael hoped Joan's plan would work and that Anna would be up to the task.

Sebastian stood up with such force his chair toppled over behind him, making Eleanor jump.

'I'm going to put a stop to this!'

'No!' Eleanor cried, 'No, Sebastian! Don't go up there, please?!' she pleaded.

'Eleanor, surely you know this is all end-of-the-pier bunkum, don't you?'

'Sebastian dear, I can't explain it but you must try and believe this is all very real. I wouldn't mislead you of all people. Let Michael do his work.'

Sebastian searched her face and knew he had lost where Eleanor was concerned and there was no point fighting her any longer. However, Anna was another matter and he lurched for the door and scrambled up the stairs.

He reached the landing and saw Anna standing just outside his bedroom. She turned and stared at him in utter panic, then looked back to Michael whose glaring eyes boring into Sebastian's could have turned blood to stone.

'Go downstairs now!' Michael bellowed.

Sebastian kept his ground while Anna looked back and forth urgently between them.

'Please...' Michael screamed but it was too late.

A sound not of this world began to echo around them, a low baying howl that grew into such intensity, that Anna put her hands to her ears and closed her eyes tight, just as Sebastian was swept off his feet with a force that got him to the bottom of the stairs without touching one of them and his head meeting with the iron handle of the front door.

Anna's high-pitched scream brought an involuntary screech from Eleanor in the kitchen, every nerve in her body startled into a spasm. She ran from the kitchen to the hallway and met Anna who had rushed down the stairs to find Sebastian curled up, a nasty bruise beginning on his brow. They both reached down and pulled him up. Still shocked and dazed, he wobbled as they led him to the sofa. They were talking to him but all he could hear was a squealing sound from the knock on his head. Eleanor and Anna stood looking at him as he started to regain his composure, then Michael called from the top of the stairs.

'Sebastian, you must tell Anna,' his voice strangely remote.

All three looked toward the stairs, then Sebastian shouted back, 'Tell her exactly what, you hideous little prick?!'

Anna recoiled at the venom.

'Why you came here,' Michael replied. It was non-reactive, matter of fact but still dream-like. 'What do you want from her?'

Sebastian stood up to lunge at Michael but both Eleanor and Anna held him back. He turned to Anna and grabbed her shoulders, 'This has to stop, Anna. This bullshit has to stop now!'

She remained calm, waiting for his anger to lessen before she spoke.

'What is it you want, Seb?'

'You know I love you,' Sebastian said in a weary voice. 'I told you that.'

'Yes, you did.'

But where there had once been affection and trust in her eyes, Anna now looked at Sebastian with mild contempt. He realised their time was over and although not the time or place he wanted to divulge such information, what the hell?

'I had hoped to ask you to marry me.'

Anna let out a small laugh and put her hand to her mouth.

'Marry?!' she exclaimed, with a mixture of incredulity and amusement.

Sebastian said nothing and took his leave, hurrying out into the garden, slamming the front door behind him. Anna started to cry as Eleanor put comforting arms around her, just as Michael called for Anna again.

'Are you all right to go, dear?' Eleanor asked.

'I have to be,' Anna replied, wiping away her tears and straightening up. Taking a deep breath, she made for the stairs.

Michael was in the middle of an incantation when she reached the doorway and watched him, fascinated rather than scared now, and noticed a faint scent of pine around her. When Michael had finished his invocation, he beckoned Anna into the room. They were the hardest steps she had taken, her legs feeling the heaviness in them from her dreams, each step toward Michael felt like she was walking through glue. As she reached him, he gently took her hand.

'Tell him to go to the light, tell him you are in the light.'

Anna couldn't find her voice as the aroma of pine became so sickly sweet she thought she might retch, then suddenly her mind was filled with vivid memories, pictures of someone else's life, of love and laughter, hopes and dreams. Anna's voice spoke with an ethereal inflection.

'Go to the light, my love, we are waiting for you in the light, we always have been. Take my hand and join us. We said *forever*.'

An airless silence followed, so complete it was as if all time had stopped and they were in a state of suspended animation. Slowly the pine scent faded and Anna began to weep.

'Are you ok, lovey?' Michael asked.

'Oh yes, I'm fine,' she replied looking at Michael, both of them with tears forming. 'They're together again. It's over.'

How Anna knew that, she didn't understand, but know it she did and with it, a lightness of being.

CHAPTER THIRTY THREE

Sebastian wandered slowly but aimlessly about the garden, occasionally glancing up at Les Dents de Lanfon and the numerous paragliders working the thermals in their composed movements.

Life was far from composed for him at that moment as he tried to come to terms with the recent events. If it were possible to feel worse, he never wished to experience it. At the very moment of triumph, it was all snatched away by matters he preferred not to dwell on anymore. For the first time all his wealth and privilege that had opened doors and brought influence, and no doubt would do so into the future, held no bearing on his most important assignment.

Sebastian could hear the words of his mother in one of her rare maternal moments, telling him as a boy that, however he achieved what he aspired to, do it honestly. Over the last few years of coming to know more about the family empire and the way in which his father, and his father before him, had built it into what it represented now, it was clear why she had counselled him so. Had he taken any notice? Was he too young at the time? Perhaps by the time he had reached an age when such an assertion would have befallen upon an understanding mind, his mother was already adrift from her parental responsibilities and seeking out the life she found with her boho set in France.

Struggling to find a niche in his father's affections, Sebastian used stealth and charm to get what he wanted which carried on into the rest of his existence. Until now, it had been a Machiavellian tool for success in his business and social life, but he had failed to see that all it might have taken to be with Anna was the honestly his mother so wisely advocated all those years ago. When life had begged him to be genuine, he had floundered. Perhaps he was now incapable of being that other person he had hoped a few weeks ago, he might become. His truth being the son of the father in totality. Well, if that were so, his father wouldn't let this set back destroy the future for him. If his heart was relegated to the back burner once again, so be it.

He had gambled and lost, now it was time to consolidate and move on.

Anna opened the front door and saw Sebastian making a forlorn figure out on the lawn. She approached him gently, placing a hand on his shoulder as he looked up at the serrated mountain that rose above them. He briefly looked round to acknowledge her but then turned his eyes back to something that had been a constant for millions of years, where everything else seemed to change like the wind.

It troubled Anna that, having already lost Max, she had now misplaced their friend as well.

'Seb?' she said softly.

'Mm?'

'I'm sorry, for everything.'

'I know, so am I,' he replied, and he seemed to relax slightly, putting an arm around Anna. 'I guess it wasn't to be and before you say anything, quite honestly I should have known better. Perhaps I should have left when I was going to, who knows?'

'We're all wise with hindsight, Seb, and I really don't want to lose you as a friend.'

'I think we both need some time to reflect on all this, don't you know?' he said, giving her shoulders a gentle squeeze. It was the kindest way he could think of to say their lives would most likely be far less complicated without each other in it.

Anna remained silent.

'If I may, I'd like to go and pack now and get back to London. Business is screaming for my attention. When you get home and only if you want to, give me a call and perhaps we can meet for supper somewhere.'

'Ok,' Anna said and with that, Sebastian gave her a light kiss on the cheek and went inside to gather his belongings.

Michael led Eleanor into each room, lighting aromatic oil burners filled with lavender. While she didn't know if she should, she said a silent prayer before leaving each room. As far as she could tell, the atmosphere everywhere had changed dramatically. This centre of so much grief was now the happy place it had once been.

After lighting the last burner, Michael took Eleanor's hand and smiled warmly. 'Eleanor, lovey, you've been marvellous.'

'But I didn't really do anything, Michael.'

'Oh, you did, believe me. You were a stabilising influence, even though you weren't aware of it. By the way, just one thing. Tell me, why do you say the Lord's Prayer?'

Eleanor looked at Michael with a raised brow and laughed, 'Michael, you are just too good!'

They hardly passed a word as Anna helped Sebastian put his bags in the car, neither knowing what to say at this stage. The boot closed with a satisfying solid thud, almost putting a full stop on the last few days and perhaps more.

'Have a safe journey,' Anna said as Sebastian opened the door. It seemed woefully inadequate.

'I will, and you take care of yourself as well,' he replied while settling himself for the drive back to London. 'Don't forget, give me a call as and when, won't you?'

'I will,' Anna said and waved as he flashed her another of his killer smiles. He watched her walking back to the house and up the stairs of the terrace, then she was gone. Sebastian sat for a moment, gathering his thoughts, after which he called a number on his phone.

'Caroline?

'Hello, stranger! Long time, no hear or see. How are you?'

'Fine, in France, on my way home.'

'Business or pleasure, darling?'

'Oh, business, always business, you know me! Hey, how about gracing me with your delicious presence tomorrow evening for supper?'

'Love to darling, our usual place?'

'Perfect, seven for drinks?'

'Super, look forward to it. Ciao, bello.'

'Ciao, gorgeous!'

Anna drove Eleanor and Michael to catch their train and the feeling in the car was much lighter than when they first arrived. In fact, Anna's whole future felt more buoyant. Before saying their goodbyes, Michael spoke with Anna about what she had been through.

"Have you experienced anything like this before, however remotely small?' Anna thought for a moment and said, 'No, just sometimes I feel my instincts were spot on but isn't that the same for everybody?

'Not really, Anna, and I believe you are naturally receptive to the spiritual realm but are unaware of it.' That rattled her senses. 'You see, nothing had happened in that house until you arrived and had you not had what we refer to as an open channel, it may never have. It's quite possible this incident has increased your ability to communicate and I'd be more than happy to help you with that, if you decide to pursue it.'

'I think I've been through enough for one lifetime, thank you, Michael!' He regarded Anna and nodded but wasn't convinced by her brusque dismissal.

Finally, they boarded the train and the first thing he would do when he got home was call Joan Golding.

Eleanor's mind was occupied by Max. She was not entirely sure her son hadn't had a hand in what happened at the house but kept that thought between herself and Max. For the first time since he had passed, she felt at peace. Helping the spirit of Armand, the experience had also laid to rest the ghost of her son. She hoped now he was finally resting in peace.

Alone once more out on the terrace, Anna absorbed the restored calm. It was time for her to leave this inexplicably beautiful place, though strangely paradoxical, a unique and priceless jewel that would sparkle in her heart for always.

Inside Anna was a new woman she needed to get acquainted with, one who didn't fit with living and working in London, this welcome significant other who wanted to broaden her horizons, to constantly learn and grow as a human being.

Carpe diem, Anna thought. *Carpe diem.*

CHAPTER THIRTY FOUR

Joyce was a whirlwind of jubilation and organisation, her daughter was coming home and staying with them before heading to London. Even Penny had picked up on an imminent arrival and kept standing on the back of a sofa, looking out of the window.

Seeing Penny on the furniture yet again, Ken decided to leave his wife to her preparations and take the dog for a long walk. It would hopefully result in Penny flopping down for a sleep by the French windows like she normally did and would prevent him getting an earful for getting in Joyce's way.

Now making the spare room up for Anna, Joyce thought about Sebastian and whether it was he who had prompted her early return. Certainly, until she knew the full measure of their relationship, Joyce wouldn't rest but it wasn't just this that kept her in an unsettled state. She had one of her 'funny feelings' about her daughter's future, as though there was an inkling of a sizable change in the air.

Anna arrived later that evening and as Ken opened the door, Penny darted out and sprinted down the driveway, skidding to a halt with a scraping of nails, then took aim and leapt into Anna's arms.

On the way home from St Pancras, Renata asked more questions in the time the journey took than Eleanor imagined possible. She kept the account fairly generic and diluted but with enough substance to indulge her insatiable companion and keep her supplied to dine out on for weeks to come.

A quick check of the time and Natalie gave Anna's desk another once over to make sure it would pass muster, just as the lady herself breezed in the entrance to the agency, looking like a different person.

'Hello, you lot,' she said with a dazzling smile they had not encountered for a long time.

'Wow, you look amazing!' Natalie gasped. 'Your hair...'

'Not too short?' Anna said, touching the new bob cut that transformed her face.

'No, it really suits you!' Natalie smiled, enviously thinking it made Anna look much younger. 'Estelle is waiting for you.'

'Yes, I am!' A theatrical voice came from the rear hallway as Estelle appeared beaming at Anna, arms outstretched for a hug. 'Look at you! Come on up and let's get some coffee.'

Finally, the small gift box from Mrs Michaels was opened and the 'just a silly thing' was in fact an elegant Cartier watch. Both Anna and Estelle were aghast.

'I can't accept this!' Anna said.

'If you don't, I will, young lady!'

'It's too small for you, anyway,' Anna joked, while fixing it around her wrist, where it fitted perfectly.

'So, come on then, tell me all about it? You're back early, why? Don't tell me you couldn't keep away from here?!'

Anna looked up from the watch and looked across the desk to Estelle, hoping what she had to tell her would be received well.

'I think I knew,' Estelle sighed when Anna had finished. 'When I saw how you looked, the new hairdo, a certain *je ne sais quoi* about you. I'm not that surprised, to be honest. Hopefully you'll stay with us until I can find a suitable replacement.'

'But you have one ready to go, Estelle. Natalie. Give her a chance.'

'I'll see but yes, she held her own while you were away. Have you any plans made yet?'

'Yes, that's the other thing, I leave in three weeks' time for California. Carmel to be exact, it's the last place I felt at one with myself so I'm going back to do the same and decide what I want to do going forward.'

Estelle smiled warmly.

'I think whatever you decide, you'll do just fine, but I for one will miss you.'

That was an understatement.

After a couple of attempts Michael finally reached Joan in her west Central Park apartment in New York where she stayed when filming her programmes. She answered in her normal sunny tones and Michael recounted the full story, Joan sometimes interjecting with a question or making an encouraging comment.

'And so that's it, warts and all, step by step, minute by minute, just how you insist.' They spoke for over an hour, during which Michael could also hear munching.

'...so all in all, Joan, I can't thank you enough for your guidance and support. I'm not sure I could have done anything like this without you.'

'Michael, I always knew you had it in you and now you've proved me right, as usual! I was more than pleased to give you input but I wasn't there, you were, so be proud of yourself, honey! Are you coming over anytime soon? I could do a whole programme on this...'

'When I've settled into my new house. Few probs with the designer but we'll get there in the end.'

'Good, Notebook will be a happy cat, he really took to you.'

'Joan?'

'Yes, honey?'

'Why do you call him *Notebook*?'

'Ah, well, you see, he listens to all my ramblings. I tell that darned cat just about everything. Honestly, if that cat could talk!'

Joan was thoughtful in the silence of her eleventh-floor apartment that looked across the famous slab of green within the city's glass and concrete jungle. When filming was over, and back in the tranquillity and seclusion of her sanctuary in Massachusetts, she would have to make contact with the kindly refined gentleman that kept riding roughshod over other spirits to get to her.

At last as the electronic sign fluttered and her gate number was revealed, Anna began the long laborious walk to her embarkation point. Her house sold in a blink of the eye, thanks to the efforts of the sales department of her old work team. In the end, Anna made the decision not to call Sebastian. Maybe one day, she would make contact but felt at ease with the possibility he was gone from her life forever.

They lifted into the air on time, Anna seated in business class, a treat to herself. As they climbed to cruising altitude, her thoughts drifted to Max. She preferred now to believe he died because it was his time and while doing something he loved and therefore, as long as she was around, Anna would be making the most of what time she had, so that when it was her time, there would be no regrets, no 'I wish I'd done that'.

When the champagne was served, Anna toasted to whatever adventures might lay ahead.

EPILOGUE

The distant echo of a droning fog horn seeped into her stirring conscious. A slow recognition of the different feel to the pillow and a gradual awareness of her surroundings preceded Anna opened her eyes. She saw her case on the floor beside the bed and vaguely remembered an exhausted rummaging for toiletries and a night shirt before collapsing into one of the two double beds. Sleep had been immediate.

After an eleven-hour flight, picking up her open-top Chrysler and driving to this Best Western hotel near the famous San Francisco waterfront, Anna had slept soundly and dreamless for nine hours. Bright sunlight glowed from behind the heavy green curtains as she yawned and stretched, feeling ravenous, and decided to indulge in a sushi breakfast at Fisherman's Wharf and then visit Pier 39, before setting off on the three-hour drive to Carmel.

Just a few minutes' walk from the hotel, Fisherman's Wharf was its usual buzzing self. After a sumptuous breakfast, in the huge Japanese restaurant on the corner directly behind the wharf's famous ship's wheel sign, Anna strolled along to Pier 39 and its numerous permanent residents. The air was filled with the unmistakably individual perfume of this particular quay. In the stillness of this typically misty morning, the mixture of sea, fish and Californian sea lion was more pungent than Anna recalled from before, but far from unpleasant and it prompted happy memories.

Still lazing from their nightly slumbers, the sea lions lolled like great lumps of brown lard on the floating pontoons, especially rigged up for them. As they lay snuggled together, maybe ten per pontoon, occasionally scratching themselves with their oddly dexterous flippers, tourists and locals alike stood and watched in silent appreciation. In this protected environment, and well over one hundred in number, they were as much a fixture of San Francisco as the ravens at the Tower of London.

An intermittent guttural barking from some of the individuals, in harmony with fog horns and sloshing of the harbour waters against the pontoons, made an amusing image, especially when one hefty sea lion rolled onto his back, scratching vigorously, and pushing another hapless animal into the water. A scrap ensued, and cameras clicked furiously.

The drive down to Carmel was thankfully uneventful, helped by the magnificent scenery spread in all directions. A couple of times, Anna caught sight of large cracks in the hillsides and knew they were the result of earth tremors, then had an internal debate whether she would want to be present during an earthquake or not, just to feel the full force of the molten iron reservoir upon which we all float.

Finally pulling to a stop in the small parking area behind the beach, Anna breathed in the sea air, her soul 'whooping' with delight, then left the car to walk down to the palest of golden sand and into the gentle arc that was the bay of Carmel. Further down the beach near the water were clumps of kelp separated from the forests in which sea otters swam with the grace of ballerinas. Where she stood, a large tree trunk lay, stripped of its bark by sand and sea water, then bleached blond by the sun. Anna sat on it, surveying the view before her, reminiscing and content that nothing seemed to have changed. She looked to the right of the bay to the peninsula that sprawled out into the ocean and the palatial home that sat perched upon the end of it like a watchful guardian. Anna pondered whether it was owned by someone incredibly famous. There were a few of Hollywood's best located in this area, particularly one Clint Eastwood, the town's mayor for a time.

With her rented studio apartment waiting, Anna took a few more moments to gaze lovingly over the Pacific Ocean. It was the same deep blue she remembered, softly undulating far out in the bay until sleepily rising up on the shallow beach shelf and commencing its superb, single curling wave along the entire beach. A perfectly timed spiralling crash of power travelling along from one end to the other, the sound and sensation nectar to the senses. She felt incomparably relaxed, thoughts soft and fluid, a state of mind she never imagined would be possible after Max died. Her breaths were slow and deep, taking it all in, feeding on the negative ions of the sea, her face lifted to the sun. She had been so right to come back, this was where she would truly be at one with herself, whoever that may end up being.

Opening her eyes, she took a last look at this small pool of a magnificent ocean as it lapped at the sand, casting her gaze along the water's edge and seeing a solitary figure walking along the shore with a small dog at heel. As the figure progressed in her direction, Anna realised it was a man, tall and dressed smartly but beach casual.

So Carmel, she mused.

He was closer now and appeared to be an older, quite distinguished man and she wondered whether maybe he was one of the select Hollywood few, then was surprised when he looked up at her sitting on the tree and lifted a hand in friendly acknowledgement. Anna happily reciprocated.

Another soft lazy thud drew her attention back to the sea and following the long wave towards her potential film star, she saw that the beach was deserted.

If you have enjoyed *Water of Life,*
read Darcy Drummond's previous novel *Summer
Season*

ABOUT THE AUTHOR

Darcy Drummond was born to show business parents and grew up surrounded by it. Although she chose not to follow them into the business, it remains a fundamental and cherished part of her life to this day. Some of the wonderful and talented people she met as a child remain her dearest friends. After having several successful careers, Darcy now concentrates on writing. She is married and lives in the south of England. This is her second novel. Her third *High Manor* will be out in the summer of 2019.

ABOUT THE PUBLISHERS

Saron Publishers has been in existence for about ten years, producing niche magazines. Our first venture into books took place in 2016 when we published *The Meanderings of Bing* by Tim Harnden-Taylor. *Minstrel Magic* by Eleanor Pritchard came out in June 2017 and tells the phenomenal show business story of the George Mitchell Singers and the Black and White Minstrels. 2018 publications included *Every Woman Remembered*, the story of the Newport women who died in service in the First World War, *From Heart and Soul,* a collection of poems by John Marshall, and *My Way*, the recollections of retired Chief Superintendent Kevin Moore.

Join our mailing list info@saronpublishers.co.uk. We promise no spam.

Visit our website saronpublishers.co.uk to keep up to date and to read reviews of what we've been reading and enjoying.

Follow us on Facebook @saronpublishers.

Follow us on Twitter @saronpublishers.

38348976R00130

Printed in Great Britain
by Amazon